Praise for Stine Pilgaard

"Pilgaard has the formidable ability to give a new twist to language and fixed expressions."
Litteratursiden

"Pilgaard has a great sense for the ironic twist hiding in any situation."
Dagbladet Information

•

Praise for The Land of Short Sentences

"Small communities love their inside jokes, which become all the more (and paradoxically) hilarious if an outsider takes them seriously. Pilgaard's smart, layered parody will make you laugh without knowing exactly why, and then will keep you laughing at your self-consciousness."
VERONICA RAIMO, author of *The Girl at the Door*

"A master of irony lays down her weapons. A deliciously crumbly novel oozing with awkward love."
Weekendavisen

"A sheer delight: Stine Pilgaard has penned a perfect comedy about normalcy."
Dagbladet Information

"*The Land of Short Sentences* comfortably won the Golden Laurels award, receiving over half the votes of Denmark's bookstores. The book of the year. An absolutely fabulous novel about adjusting to midlife in the back of beyond."
Jyllands-Posten

"Stine Pilgaard has a pronounced talent for parody. She can write in such a way as to make you laugh out loud, bringing our embarrassments out into the open, capturing the absurdities of everyday life. Her dialogues are natural and precise, her language clear and succinct, and her references plain and recognizable. But beneath the lightness of her prose hides something beyond comedy and rhetoric."
Berlingske

"Another Pilgaard pearl. Too funny for words and at the same time so keenly intelligent in its depictions. You love her characters to bits and understand their faltering steps on the road to community so well. A book you'll cherish reading—again and again and ..."
SØNDAG

"Stine Pilgaard's crisp prose and supreme timing can be spotted fifty books away. It's an exquisite pearl of a book, wonderfully funny, playful, and subtle in its crafting. But don't be mistaken: beneath the humor there's a worldly-wise voice with a finely honed ability to put into words all that's profound and beautiful and good about life. This is one of the best works of Danish literature I've read in ages."
Litteratursiden

"*The Land of Short Sentences* is a tragicomic genre hybrid including advice columns, *højskole* songs, and a thoroughly maladapted, infinitely charming narrator. The book's disasters are small, and it is a situational comedy that gives us a break from world events. But it is not cozily escapist or trivial; it is a consolation, a reminder of something common, comical, and troublesome that persists while dramatic global events take place: the fact that people need people, no matter how awkward it can

be. Dear Stine Pilgaard. I would like to say congratulations on the award, but also: thank you for the book. Because it made it a little easier to live, without lying about it being easy. Because it lingered with irresistible joy on all the little inconveniences that make up the social landscape. Because it made it much easier to be a weirdo who ventures across the boundaries of others with the best of intentions."
LINEA MAJA ERNST, *Weekendavisen*

"Pilgaard has written an entertaining parody of the rural idyll. With dry Danish humor she describes the difficult integration of a woman in West Jutland. The problems that men and women of all ages spew into the letter section are all too recognizable. Divorces, alcoholism, jealousy and work addiction, everything is discussed."
De Volkskrant

"What an absolutely wonderful book."
Het Parool

"Pilgaard is one of the most talented writers in Denmark. In the mildly satirical *The Land of Short Sentences*, she provides both entertainment and depth. The book is a sharp diagnosis of Scandinavian modern-family resentment and of outrageous idealism and social alienation."
De Morgen

"Sharp, observant, entertaining, and empathetic. The novel's greatness is that it does not rely on tricks or shortcuts, but only warmhearted storytelling and an incredible ability to capture a scene."
Modernista, Swedish publisher

"Stine Pilgaard writes tenderly and wittily about the agonies of learning to drive and being a parent, of living on an island and among other people, in an imperfect present and a self-created future. It's the perfect read for our time."
Kanon Verlag, German publisher

"The Land of Short Sentences is funny, tender, surprising. It is a novel that makes you laugh out loud and then touches you deeply in the next moment. There are beautiful observations about how people live their lives, observations about parenthood, community, relationships. Just like its main character, the Letterbox (!), the novel is quirky, funny, a bit crazy, but so very loveable!"
WSOY, Finnish publisher

•

Praise for Lejlighedssange ("Songs for Special Occasions")

"Read this book if you want an experimental and challenging read full of exquisite prose and humor."
Litteratursiden

"Contains a colorful gallery of characters."
Berlingske

"Although it is a captivatingly easy read and unpretentious, there is plenty of artistic design, compositional creativity, and literary reference at play. It all fits together seamlessly, as the form and content of this novel form a beautiful whole."
Dagbladet Information

The Land
of Short
Sentences

Stine Pilgaard
The Land
of Short
Sentences

Translated from the Danish
by Hunter Simpson

WORLD EDITIONS
New York, London, Amsterdam

Published in the USA in 2022 by World Editions LLC, New York
Published in the UK in 2022 by World Editions Ltd., London

World Editions
New York | London | Amsterdam

Meter i sekundet
Copyright © Stine Pilgaard and Gutkind Forlag A/S, København, 2020
Published by agreement with Winje Agency A/S, Norway
English translation copyright © Hunter Simpson, 2022
Author portrait © Alexander Banck-Petersen
Cover illustration © Annemarie van Haeringen

Printed by Lake Book, USA

World Editions is committed to a sustainable future. Papers used by World
Editions meet the FSC standards of certification.

Library of Congress Cataloging in Publication Data is available

ISBN 978-1-64286-108-2

Translation of this book was supported by the Danish Arts Foundation

Danish Arts
Foundation

Twitter: @WorldEdBooks
Facebook: @WorldEditionsInternationalPublishing
Instagram: @WorldEdBooks
YouTube: World Editions
www.worldeditions.org

Book Club Discussion Guides are available on our website.

To the memory of Maja Trappaud Ahlgren Westmann

with closed eyes

it is as though
no current can drown me
no sorrow strangle me
completely —
it is as though
love comes to me
across all oceans
because a soft string always sways
within me —

Gustaf Munch-Petersen, *the low land*, 1933

WE ARE STILL new to these fields, and we walk through them with our baby carriage in a state of confusion, like two restless vagabonds. We look up at the windmills, the way they appear against the sky like visitors from a distant time, futuristic souvenirs from other planets. They shoot up around our house like cheerful weeds, and, on the rare occasions they stand still, it's as if the globe is holding its breath for a short second, bewildered by the wind's absence. We drift through a new world, in our new life, with our new child. Nature lies flat before us, and the sunset over the North Sea considers us with its red eye. Deer stare calmly into headlights, and dead animals lie in repose between the road's stripes. The farmers greet us with one finger raised to their caps, which, I gather, is how it's done here. Waving, smiling, rolling, I move through the corn and potatoes, the rye and wheat. I feign interest in my neighbors' dogs. How old is it, I say, which breed, a labrador, how nice, such reliable dogs. I admire the dialect of West Jutland, its ungrammatical insistence on tradition, the fjord that glints like shards of glass in the sun. Trucks transporting windmill parts balance along the roadways, a blade grazes an oncoming car, traffic weaves its way through the landscape, takes a bow, thanks the crowd, and disappears again. *We Want It in Velling*, the town's welcome sign announces, but what we want isn't exactly clear. Reality lies around us like a fog, and we've only just arrived.

Nature Plus the Present Tense

THE PRINCIPAL KNOCKS three times in quick succession and lets herself in. That's how we do it out here, she says when I look up at her in surprise. Doesn't anyone in Velling have sex, I ask, isn't there anyone who watches porn or masturbates, you can't get your clothes on after just three knocks. People manage, says the principal, and she takes two cups from the cabinet. She has bought a bag of black tea and a little sieve for herself, because she doesn't care for my Pickwick. That's a coffee drinker's tea, she says, only one step above Medova, and no one wants to go there. She's just been over at the *højskole* to put flowers in the students' rooms. Before long, they'll be arriving in blue buses from across the country. Farewell tranquility, I say, and soon I'll have to bid farewell to my maternity leave as well. The principal rotates her cup slowly between her hands while my son hides under her red dress as if it were a tent. He needs a name, the principal says, pointing between her legs. She says people are starting to talk. She has contacts in local government, and she knows that they've already sent us three fines. You sound like a mafia boss, I say. The principal lifts our son up and he reaches out for the plastic flower on her hair clip. Are you a little Nicolai, she asks. My son drools indifferently. A name is a big responsibility, I say. A sequence of letters that school teachers will yell out every day when they go down the list. A name our son will say every single time he meets another person. At playgrounds, nightclubs, and job interviews. He'll sign documents with the name we come up with. It will sit in the top corner of the drawings we hang on the refrigerator. It will be scratched into the ugly clay pots that we get as Christmas gifts, and it will end its days on a headstone. In the interim it will appear in medical records, on academic examinations, rental agreements, bank loans, Christmas cards, criminal records, and possibly Wikipedia. You have no idea where your name will end up, I say. The principal suggests Frederik. I reject it out of hand, because my first criterion is that it has to be rhymeable. For his confirmation, I say, and the major birthdays, we have the chance right now to make it easy on ourselves. Severin, says the principal, rhymes with bedouin. I'm not sure how often I'll be able to use that one, I say. We're looking for something with two syllables ending in a vowel sound, so we've come that far. You need to get out of your little bubble, the principal says. In the year that we've lived in Velling, I've done nothing but throw up, give birth, and breast-feed. My son smiles at me as if none of these three activities have anything to do with him. He needs a name, says the principal, and you need a job. It's about integration, all of our experience shows that the school's teachers only continue living here if their spouses find a way to settle in. We're not married, I say. You ought to see to that, says the principal, and she points to my son as if the matter required no further discussion. She harbors the province dweller's fear that new families will vanish just as the local community is blossoming. In her free time the principal finds romantic partners for people so they won't move away. She herself was hired as a dance teacher during the school's summer session, and she was only meant to stay here for four weeks. That was thirty years ago now, and that's how it goes for plenty of people, she says, this place has an attraction that makes it inconceivable to leave. And it's the teachers and their trailing spouses who create the school's story, says the principal. All of the teachers live with their families in residences around the big red-brick building, as if it were a church, the natural center of a hysterical religious community. You are the school, says the principal, pointing at me. Her voice rises and falls, paints pictures and broadcasts advertisements. There's a farm with a little roadside shop on the way to Højmark where you can just drop by and leave money on the counter and everything's a hundred percent organic. The town is brimming with entrepreneurs and idealists, and so many vegetarians you can't swing a dead cat without hitting one. It's not just mink farms and evangelical churches out here. The farmers know about more than just their crops, and the fishermen don't only talk about fish. So, the principal says as she takes off her glasses, where do your talents lie. Her eyes are glowing turquoise, and the lamp over the table sways back and forth in her left iris. I'm a sort of oracle, I say, but hardly anybody knows it. An oracle, mumbles the principal, and she looks like someone trying to solve a complicated problem of foreign diplomacy. I can tell that she is the one who keeps the town together, and perhaps the whole country. She gently pulls some strings, tugs a little harder if necessary, and in the blink of an eye she's relocated a few sand dunes and there are ocean views for all. We need youthful ener-gies here, says the principal, and she gives me a job that doesn't exist and for which I haven't applied. She arranges it all, studying me penetratingly while mak-ing a couple of quick, whispered phone calls. That was the newspaper, says the principal, and it turns out that they could use an advice column aimed at all age groups. I lift my son into his playpen. A lot of people do the wedding at the same time as the baptism, says the principal, two birds, one stone. He's not going to be baptized, I say. The principal nods slightly to herself and says, We'll think about that further down the line. She leaves her tea and her sieve in the top drawer. So it's here for next time, she says. Thank you, I say, and I roll a yellow ball toward my son. We want it in Velling, says the principal. Yes we do, I say.

Dear Letterbox,

I'm writing to you because I have a problem with time, and a number of my closest friends and family have made comments about it. I'm really bad at living in the present, and I'm often a few weeks ahead in my thoughts. I'm used to planning a lot in my job as a coordinator at a big company. On the home front there is a lot to manage because we have three children, what with school events, extracurricular activities, and everything that entails. My husband is very absentminded and he often double- or triple-books us. This has led both his family and friends to come to me whenever something needs to be arranged. You'll have to consult the Sorceress of the Schedules, my husband will say, and even though I'm sure he means it with love, I can't help but take it as a criticism. I try to be present. I meditate and I listen to dolphin sounds, but I must admit that it doesn't come naturally to me. Am I a control freak? What should I do?

Sincerely,

The Scheduling Sorceress

Dear Scheduling Sorceress,

This isn't supposed to be about me, but I freely admit that I'm the type of person who has a hard time getting things done. This is owing not to a spontaneous approach to life, but rather a mix of laziness and indecision. Personally, I think the present is overrated. Live every day as if it were your last, they say, but that's a bunch of nonsense. For god's sake, don't do that. The streets would be deserted, no one would take responsibility for anything. People would stay in bed all day with their lovers, smoking cigarettes and calling their parents to forgive them. I'm so tired of the present, you're always right in the middle of it. It's now and now and, heaven help me, now as well. There's no crime in thinking about tomorrow. If you want to get together with your family or friends, you have to understand that it doesn't happen by chance. You don't just walk into a café and suddenly find them all sitting around talking about the good old days. I have a friend called Mathias who loves to organize things, it puts him into a state of euphoria. Mathias is initiative made flesh, and he progresses through life from one goal to the next. With a flick of the wrist he composes long emails about tiny details. When no one responds, he sends reminders with smiley faces, attaches weather forecasts, and makes suggestions as to appropriate attire. I'm not sure why we always tease Mathias, but it must be because it's so easy to do. Like so many others, my boyfriend and I are people of leisure. We walk into parties as though the world had been discovered just for us. Every group of friends has its leisure people. You'll recognize us because we only ever bring chips or a bottle of schnapps to social gatherings. We are very sensitive, and we RSVP at the last moment. We feel like life is confining if we have too many plans lined up. We perceive time in the abstract, something with a will of its own. It's difficult for us to understand something which is, for others, readily apparent: no planning, no holiday party. It's a meaningful thing to decorate and to arrange transportation for others. We arrive with a crooked smile, and, because we have a guilty conscience, we are a little bit mean. Whoa there, cowboy, we say to Mathias, or, Hakuna matata. But there is something worth remembering. There's a reason why it was two cartoon characters who taught us that phrase. Our world wasn't created by Walt Disney. The stars don't arrange themselves into the head of a lion who can tell us who we are. But you can. Dear Scheduling Sorceress, and dear Mathias, I'm sorry. People with big hearts are always teased. Keep your spirits high, fill my calendar, waste my time. Your plans and dreams are the maypoles the rest of us dance around. After the party we'll all go home, back to our busy lives, and you'll be left to do the cleaning up while you think about how it might be fun to rent canoes and row down Gudenå River in the summer of '22. From the bottom of my heart, I thank you.

Warm regards,

The Letterbox

I'VE ORDERED A manual to go along with my driving lessons, and I walk over to the grocery store to pick up the package. I know exactly who you are, the grocer says when I hand him my ID. Is that right, I say. He nods. And I know where you live, he says, down by the school in the little red house. Right again, I say. He leans against the doorframe, and I start to feel overwhelmed by all of the options in the bulk candy section. Cars pass by outside, and the grocer lifts his hand toward his temple. It doesn't quite reach, but I think about how he must carry out that same motion, hand to almost-temple, around a hundred times per day. How can you possibly tell who it is, I say. It never hurts to wave to somebody you don't know, the grocer says, as if he's confessing to something. He asks whether we've settled in. I'd like to be friends with this grocer, and I fantasize about him dropping by for a visit in the evenings. We could listen to music and drink wine together, laugh at the things we say to one another. You get knocked back to square one, I say, and you've got to rediscover yourself in your new surroundings. I talk about how moving turns you into a foreigner, and the grocer starts rearranging some products. When I talk to people I'm like someone setting off to war. I become too eager, and, alone in a soup of sounds, I lie down before them like a sliced pork roast on a platter, a melting ice-cream sundae stuck with silly umbrellas. The grocer looks out the window, clearly hoping for reinforcements, when a middle-aged couple steps into the store. They live in Hee, but they shop here regularly because their children go to the charter school in Velling. Their conversation wanders slowly and cautiously through a little landscape, enthusiastically taking up residence in the least dangerous places. A heavy rainstorm, fall vacations, which are just around the corner, any statement to which it would be impossible to object. For the better part of ten minutes they stand at the counter, agreeing with one another's every word. The couple have just cleaned out their garage. You gather so much junk over the years, it's just got to be done. Right, yeah, true, the grocer says, and I'm filled with a mix of fasci nation and disgust at his ability to agree with them three times in one sentence. It seems like the others are getting closer to one another, while I feel like I'm being pushed farther and farther away, out toward an abyss of loneliness. Once the couple have walked out the door with four marzipan frogs from the display case, I put a paper bag full of candy up on the counter. Good manners make me paranoid, I say as I find my wallet in my bag, you can never tell what lies on the other side of a mountain. That'll be 188.50, says the grocer. Maybe you think about things too much. I probably do, I say, and I leave the shop while the phantom grocer, laughing in my kitchen over a glass of red wine, dissolves into small, flickering specks.

AT HOME IN my living room I have a cry over my conversational woes. I'm going to end up like a cat lady without any cats, I sob. My boyfriend tells me I've got to understand that the grocer isn't rejecting me, he's just adhering to the rules of a genre. You think in prose, he says, but people here are more concise. Like haiku, says my boyfriend, who compares everything to literature. Seven syllables, nature plus the present tense. He frequently employs his intellect as a shield against my big feelings, and if I'm lucky then I get a lecture thrown into the bargain. It's not as complicated as you think, says my boyfriend, who is from a small town. Conversations in public spaces reinforce the imposed community that is a rural village. But the grocer asked me himself if we had settled in, I say. My boyfriend wags his finger and shakes his head. Wrong, he says, the grocer acknowledged that you happened to be in his store, and that you both live in the same place. When my boyfriend thinks I'm being particularly dense, his metaphors grow desperate and florid. Two lions from the same pride meet on the savannah over a dying zebra, he says slowly. They take a couple of bites, and the zebra's back left leg twitches gently. Afterwards, they both go their own way, but they know that they might perhaps meet again over the same cadaver in a few days' time. Think of your interactions as a nursery rhyme, says my boyfriend, a short ritual. How's it going, it's going fine. What a windy day, it sure is. Looks like it's Monday again, there's no escaping it. I repeat the phrases slowly, like magic spells I don't really believe in. My boyfriend advises me to repress my need for intimacy, or at least hide it a little better. Take Anders Agger, he knows how to talk to everybody, my boyfriend says, searching online for his documentaries. We go into the kitchen to make popcorn. What's up, he says, pouring it into a big bowl. Nothing much, I mumble, and we sit down on the sofa to practice. How's it going, says my boyfriend. Fine thanks, I answer. Did you have a good weekend, he asks. I say that it's always nice to wind down after a busy week. My boyfriend nods encouragingly. No one really wants to know how you're doing, he says, remember that.

Dear Letterbox,

My husband and I have been married for over a decade and we have four wonderful dogs. We live in a beautiful area a little ways outside of Vedersø. We're both employed, and we don't have anything to complain about, but my husband thinks a lot about how we can improve our lives. When I lie down in bed after a long day, he sometimes looks at me and says, are you really happy? Then I get even more tired than I already was. My husband is afraid that we've stopped evolving as a couple, that we don't challenge one another anymore. I'm not worried, though I am getting a bit exhausted. Maybe I have low expectations, but I'm grateful for our life together. Do you have any suggestions for how my husband can learn to find peace?

Sincerely,

David

Dear David,

I acknowledge your exhaustion, but it's important that you understand the mechanisms that are driving your husband. Not everyone is good at being happy. Some people get restless, and others feel insecure. My in-laws belong to a clan of grocers from Fyn, and food products are their passion. They like to discuss the merits of Brugsen's different supermarkets. LocalBrugsen is the black sheep of the bunch, DailyBrugsen parts the seas, but SuperBrugsen is beyond all compare. They all work there together, and my boyfriend's grandmother has even produced a series of ceramic tea sets with Super-Brugsen's initials glazed onto the cups. It says SB on the side, and whenever the family gets together, they pour their coffee into these cups and raise them in a toast. I love my in-laws, but I thrive best in disharmony, among sick people. It is in the world of misunderstanding that I feel most at home. I sense conflict the way others breathe in air. I analyze shifts in tone automatically, I perceive the sharpness around the edges of a voice. Hurt feelings, an offended curl of the lips, tightening jaws, raised eyebrows. I can smooth things over and resolve disagreements in the most subtle of ways. In fact, I ought to make a career out of it. My big grief is that normal families have no need of my services. Beneath my smile, I search for signs of danger. I lie in wait, ready to rescue them from something that will never come. Any thought of divorce is distant as a Russian village, and positivity exudes from the living room furniture. Every Christmas we travel to my boyfriend's ancestral home. We daughters-in-law core the apples to cook along with the pork belly, we arrange cheese platters with red and yellow bell peppers, and we fold napkins adorned with happy elves. I pull myself together and try to fit in as best I know how. You can do it, I whisper to myself. You are as impassive and pale as a statue. You are a gilt-framed painting in your grandmother's dining room, you are the deer and the forest lake, the undulating water lilies. You are IKEA, a hysterically zoomed-in photo of a flower's crown of petals, dewdrops in the sunshine, millions of reproductions. You are so neutral that you hang in hotel rooms the world over. You are the last thing people see before they sink into the bathtub and slice open their veins, and you fit in every home. Dear David, that is my little mantra, and maybe it would work for your husband. Show mercy. Harmony doesn't come naturally to everyone.

Warm regards,

The Letterbox

MY BOYFRIEND AND I are outside of the house in Velling where we've signed our son up for daycare. We have a meeting with the woman who runs it, and we park our bicycles in the carport. Candles burn in little lanterns in the windows, and there's a wreath with red berries hanging on the door. We've donned presentable outfits for the occasion, and we smile as we shake hands with the middle-aged woman who greets us. She gestures to a wooden bench in the kitchen and we take a seat. We didn't discuss it beforehand, but I think we're both unsure whether it's her or us who is getting hired today. The woman introduces herself as Maj-Britt, and she tells us that she's had the daycare for thirty-two years. She's an old hand, says her husband, poking his head into the kitchen. Why thank you, Bent, Maj-Britt says as she pours the coffee. Maj-Britt, I say, that's the Danish name with the most different spellings. I sense a rush of excitement. Hyphenated with a double *t*, she says, and she takes out a weekly schedule with little ladybugs drawn in the corners. She explains that she runs a green daycare with a special emphasis on connecting with nature. The funny thing, I say, is that the name is actually quite short, and yet both syllables are filled with possibilities: *ai*, *j*, or *y*, single or double *t*, with or without an *h*, there are infinite variations. Not quite infinite, says my boyfriend, and he begins to do the calculations on his phone. We shift the letters of her name into different formations and I take notes on a napkin. Twenty-seven, says my boyfriend. He thinks that the second part of the name probably stems from the Celtic "Birgitte," meaning brilliant or exalted one.

Spell it however you like, I'll know who you mean, Maj-Britt says. She asks us if we've settled in here in West Jutland. My boyfriend gives me a stern look. We can't complain, I say. There's a big RV parked out in the front yard, and as Bent pours our coffees he tells us that they normally keep it parked in Tarm, but once a year they fill up the tank and take all the kids out for a ride. Maj-Britt shows us some pictures of what a typical day at the daycare looks like, and she wants to know if we have any questions for her. I rack my brains, feeling like we ought to have some well-defined notions about the place where our son is going to spend his next few years. It'll go by quickly, says Maj-Britt, and before you know it you'll be taking him to preschool. I agree with her that it's crazy how much they grow, especially when you consider that the initial production time is just ten or fifteen minutes. Maybe half an hour, I say with a laugh, if fortune smiles. My boyfriend clears his throat, and I add in a serious voice that we're doing battle with a bit of diaper rash at the moment. It won't stand a chance against us, says Maj-Britt, as if we've just become allied in war. She tells us about a special zinc ointment that she orders from Sweden, and I experience a momentary feeling of success. What do two young people such as yourselves do for a living, Bent asks us. My boyfriend tells them about his teaching job at the højskole, and I say that I'm in the oracle industry. I see, Maj-Britt says. She has an advice column, my boyfriend clarifies. So we can always come to you for a bit of friendly guidance, says Bent, and I assure him that he can. Maj-Britt and my boyfriend start talking about the weather in Velling. I've prepared for this scenario at home, and I grasp for my knowledge of average temperatures and typical cloud formations. It doesn't sound as authentic as I had hoped, but Maj-Britt appears satisfied. Well, it seems like we're all done here, says Bent, and I get the feeling that we've been approved. Once we're outside with our bicycles, we turn to one another. How do you think it went, my boyfriend asks. I shrug my shoulders. It's become an absolute given that, in situations where we need to seem like parents, we talk as if we've been acting or taking some sort of test. Good thinking with the diaper rash, he says.

THE HØJSKOLE FACULTY are out in the parking lot to greet the fall semester's new students, and I stand at the window, assessing the situation. The students start to turn up, either in buses or dropped off by their parents. They look either cocky or shy as they ask one another where they're from, and which subjects they're signed up for. I station myself in the smoking area at the school's entrance, and I feel like I'm at the theater. Some of the students have already decided who they'll become at the school, and I try to spot the ones who seem to diverge most from their original personalities. There is an exaggerated quality to their body language that amuses me. None of them are at ease, and I prefer that the ones who aren't trying too hard to hide it. A young man with thick curls drums with his fingertips on the tabletop. Are you studying music, I ask. He nods and offers me his hand. Malte, he says with a serious voice. I tell him I'm in the oracle industry, and that he can always come to me if he has any problems. He takes the cigarette that I offer him. The music students tend to settle in quickly, I say, they seek each other out and form bands with names like Funky McFunkins and Lord of the Strings. In the first two weeks they use the band names ironically, but as the semester goes on, they start saying them in the same way you'd talk about The Beatles or The Rolling Stones. Nearby, a black-haired girl with bright-red lipstick is glaring at an ashtray as if it had committed some sort of grievous bodily harm against her. The writing students smoke constantly. They shiver out in the cold with haunted expressions on their faces. As the creative writing teacher, my boyfriend gets a lot of the so-called demanding students, who, like everyone who writes, feel a compulsion to explain themselves and harbor a vague expectation that the written word will be their salvation. They are children of divorced parents with high grade averages, there is a prevalence of depression and bipolar disorder among them, and there are always a few aspiring journalists mixed in with a strong sense of justice. In a few weeks they'll be turning up at our front door one by one with a hazy intuition that my boyfriend has the answer to something they want to find out. They'll drink black coffee in his office and smoke cigarettes, usually my boyfriend's. Is there something you want to talk about, my boyfriend will ask, and I'll fall asleep to the voice of a muddled young person who doesn't know whether it's a father, a brother, a lover, or a friend that they're hoping to find. The principal comes waltzing over in a long, purple dress, her long hair piled creatively atop her head. There's a whirling quality to her movements, her dress billows like wings, and it wouldn't be imprecise to say that she was flying. She corrals the students like a flock of sheep down to the assembly hall, where she leads them in a folk dance. They stomp across the floor bashfully to the principal's commands. Most of them have just finished high school, and they come to the højskole in the hope that they'll find the sense of meaning they've been searching for. They make up their minds that they will on the way here, and their letters home are written before they even arrive, as sure as the sun rises in the east. The højskole is a concentrate, a bouillon cube of dreams. Dreams of a community that can be sung, danced, and talked into being. They pay money to be in this setting, and they know that everyone around them is after the same experience. There is, therefore, something self-fulfilling and silly about their little universe. Because they long for friendship, they pretend to be friends, until they in fact become friends. They forge powerful bonds in no time at all, saying things like that's so you and it's an inside joke within a matter of weeks. There are always a handful of slightly older students with a tendency to pontificate. They've either read too many books or are taking a break from their university studies in the humanities, and, consequently, they bear witness to the community from the outside, with painful yet triumphant contempt. Some of them coldly scrutinize the school's artificial environment. They always live in single rooms and they never sign up for choral groups. Although I'm most similar to these students in their single rooms, I like the others better. I envy them their joyous abandon, the way they let themselves go. One day they will become fantastic parents and citizens, and in their romantic relationships they will, with open eyes and tranquil minds, entrust themselves entirely to the people they have decided to share their lives with.

Dear Letterbox,

I am a sixty-seven-year-old woman, and I think getting older is strange. Personally, I don't feel like my own outlook on life has changed, but I've noticed that, like society at large, the people closest to me have started to treat me differently. Ever since I retired it's been hard to carry on conversations at social gatherings. I have four lovely grandchildren, but I can't talk about them all the time, and when the conversation runs dry I end up confirming people's prejudices about my grandmotherly age. I'm also a bit confused as to why so many men seem to want to touch or squeeze my upper arm. Why do you think they're doing that?

Sincerely,

The Youthful Elder

Dear Youthful Elder,

I was twenty-six the first time a man told me that I was aging well. When I happen to mention my age, I often find myself being reassured that it doesn't show, which is, by the way, a lie. I've always looked older than I really am. As a child I was proud of it, as a teenager it was practical, and now I just don't care. It's endlessly exasperating to have the desire to look younger projected onto me, to be perceived as a food product with an expiration date. It is confounding to be a woman. At puberty we are bestowed with a power we can hardly understand as we contemplate our budding breasts. We plod along in their wake, somewhat perplexed, batting away the fingers that reach out to touch them. But fatigue sets in, and you think: Good Lord. For a few years we are the object of society's desire. We are blank pages, the opposite of death. Like everyone, we confuse youth with eternity, and we are baffled when we discover that it was only ours on loan. We end up with no fingers to bat away, at most a couple of hungry children, and the gaze of society grows sentimental. It drifts from our breasts to our bellies, before creeping down into the baby carriage, where it thanks us with a smile for our contribution to the human race. For a short period of time we are handled with care, treated like ambassadors of Mother Earth herself. Dear Youthful Elder, men operate best in relation to the female body when something is either going into it or coming out of it. When that's all over and done with, the situation gets critical. Discombobulation descends upon them. In utter confusion and with a total lack of imagination, they cling to your upper arms. Good Lord.

Sincerely,

The Letterbox

I MEET UP with Krisser at the pedestrian street and we proceed through Ringkøbing behind our baby carriages. Judging from our bags, you would take us for two women heading out on a round-the-world expedition. After less than a year as mothers, the majority of our vocabulary consists of nouns defining the objects that we drag around with us. Zinc salves, ring slings, diaper bags, and baby alarms. I see it as a victory of compound words and a wretched defeat of our language. Our homes are invaded by diaper pails, wet wipes, high chairs, playpens, and sippy cups. These are words I had never before uttered, and they still feel awkward as they pass through my mouth. Like the confused first blowjob of a much-too-young girl, it's uncomfortable for all involved. Krisser passes me a soggy paper cup. She shakes her head in annoyance, and makes an expression of sorrow and disgust. Is it bad again, I ask, and she nods. Krisser exists in a world that is constantly offending her sensibilities, and I secretly love the pained faces she makes. Her eyes turn into two gloomy chasms, and her pursed lips tremble pitifully in the air. You'd think she was being force-fed shit or vomit, the puss of an infected wound, or the yellow-green snot of an autumnal cold, when in fact she's been served a caffe latte at the wrong temperature. Her daughter looks on with concern from beneath her green bonnet, and I stroke her cheek. Krisser takes a deep breath, as if she has decided to give the world another chance, while at the same time despising herself for this folly. Her face slowly falls back into place, and she again resembles the pretty porcelain doll I had as a child. Krisser has signed us up for The Loop, a gym that offers circuit training classes. She's not really into fitness and wellness, but she thinks we need to get in shape. When we met for the first time in our mothers' group, Krisser and I stared at one another as if we were castaways, flailing and gasping on the open sea, who had just spotted another person floating by. We ate mountains of the pastries which were piled before us like ammunition, ours for the taking. Dagmar pies, pretzels, Skagen horns, cookie cakes, cinnamon buns, chocolate balls, and truffles. We talked about our genitalia, compared stretch marks, and pulled out our breasts, saying: Sorry if I leak. My boyfriend was at the højskole, Karsten was at the hotel, and when our children's eyes opened, it was to us they looked in expectation. Google withdrew in defeat and abandoned us in a world full of bodies. Our long conversations could be boiled down to one single, burning question: Is this normal. Normal was the new black, normal was a check mark, normal was a thick vine hanging in the jungle that could swing you across a river of lurking crocodiles. We hoped for average levels of crying, neither too much nor too little, to thread the needle between colicky wailing and stone-cold silence. Although our children were growing all the time, we could not fully grasp that they were actually getting bigger, that there would be an end to the nights of breastfeeding. That they would one day rise up off the carpet and walk, lift up a knife and fork and eat their own food from a plate, sit down on the toilet and reach out for toilet paper. Too tired to remember a before or to believe in an after, we melted into an eternal present. Bodily fluids flowed between us, milk, sweat, and tears. Our stitches were tight, our breasts swollen. We were a bow and arrow of flesh: we breathed in and all was aquiver, and when we exhaled our contours suddenly vanished. With absolutely no preparation, we had been sucked into a universe filled with cheerful illustrations and singing teddy bears. Krisser wasn't happy, but she was fun, and we solved our problems in the same way. Like the cogs of a gear, we clung to each other in desperation, we pumped out our breast milk, and got Krisser's father-in-law to drive us to Biergarten in Søndervig. The servers were young women dressed in the traditional costume of the German Alps. They looked ready for Oktoberfest, and their breasts were miraculous. Baby-blanketbreastpumpplaymat, we yelled, and the one who stumbled over the words first had to get the next round. We told each other stories of life before children, and we became wilder and more fun in our anecdotes than we ever were in reality. You should've known me before I got pregnant, Krisser said, it's a shame you have to settle for the remnants. I can make her out through the cracks of motherhood, but I wish we had an authentic archive of memories that we could reminisce about together. I feel like I missed out on knowing her in my youth, like there is a little Krisser-shaped hole in my past. One too few guests at my birthday parties, an empty seat in the train cars of my Interrail trip. We should have played darts in Florence, should have imbibed Aperol Spritzes in Rome and painted the town red. That was back when I was going to be a prizewinning journalist and Krisser a singer in a rock band, back when we believed that anything could happen, long before the present tense, where suddenly our eyes have met, right in the middle of reality.

IT'S SATURDAY, AND there is a singing marathon at the højskole. The music teacher has planned an homage to the *Højskole Songbook*, so from nine in the morning until nine at night, all the students and teachers will be sitting in the assembly hall united in song. In the breaks there will be presentations about the association between music and community. That's one way to spend your weekend, says Sebastian, who is married to the ceramics teacher. We're standing with our children, looking in through the windows of the assembly hall. The singers look grotesque, because you can't hear their voices, but you can see their distorted faces, their jaws loosening and clenching, their mouths opening and closing in unison. The højskole is a force of nature, a lover you can't hope to compete with, and Sebastian and I are bitter. We both have partners who have been sucked into the school's climate-controlled womb. The principal thinks it's important for us trailing spouses to be a part of everyday life at the højskole. It's about the students' sense of continuity, she wrote in an email to Sebastian and me. We were encouraged to hold spontaneous lectures for the students about subjects that interest us, and to come in as guest teachers when the school's faculty are away at workshops or retreats. It's a cult, says Sebastian, and they're trying to pull us in. When all of the teachers went to a seminar on Grundtvig, the two of us led the morning assembly. The students were courteous, but they knew that we didn't truly love them, that we were just two friendly but transitory au pairs. They're singing off-key, Sebastian says, and he looks as though someone has hurt his feelings. He's a composer, and recently he's been inspired by everyday clamor. He records the noises of his wife's pottery wheel, her feet against the wooden floor, knives scraping metal, the strange, sucking sounds of wet hands working with clay. It sounds like the sex scene from *Ghost*, I say, but he sees his music as an alternative to that kind of popular culture. He has just finished mixing a track consisting of the sound vibrations made by him flicking his fingers against the edge of a ceramic bowl. Sebastian's daughter gently knocks on a windowpane of the assembly hall, where everyone is now standing in a circle holding hands. Can you believe that we're letting our children grow up here, he says, how did we even consider uprooting them from the city. I tell Sebastian that we should write some new højskole songs, that we should form a teacher band. We're not teachers, he says, but all the same, he bends down to get his ceramic bowl, which he has in Freja's stroller. He hums a little melody and glides his fingers along the edge of the bowl. No, I say, we're making protest songs, and for that we need a guitar.

Battle Hymn of the Trailing Spouses
Protest Song

Melody: When I See a Red Flag Flying
(Når jeg ser et rødt flag smælde)
Composer: Johannes Madsen, 1923

1 It is hard to be a teacher
   everybody would agree
   but perhaps it's even bleaker
   to look on from the periphery
   we've trailed our spouses for so long
   that we've nearly lost our way
   and we don't know if we belong
   on the trails that our spouses say.

2 You can spend your life awandering
   like an exhausted pilgrim
   through the gloomy darkness, pondering
   why the trail should be so lonesome
   there's no space for us in sunshine
   we do the shopping, and all the chores
   in the shadow of the school we pine
   for some happiness and nothing more.

3 Like the fans of a star athlete
   who gets all the love and glory
   we cheer and wave and massage his feet
   and pay the price for his victory
   we offer comfort when he is weary
   but after the game it's all too clear
   that when we are feeling dreary
   our hero, he is nowhere near.

4 They may disregard our strife
   but our army's on the march
   we're the extras in the theater of life
   and no one shall stop our charge
   for we are the trailing spouses
   in the North Sea's wind we'll prevail
   or perhaps we'll look around us
   and find a different trail.

THE LESSON IS over and there's an awkward silence in the car. Since I passed the written test I've been taking so-called experience hours. I go to driving lessons the way other people go golfing. Last week my bank called with concerns about all of the transfers I've been making, referring to them as suspicious. Fifty-eight payments, said the bank's representative, and I could tell that she was wondering if I was a victim of blackmail. Nice, nice, says my driving instructor, a friendly man from Søndervig who likes to give high fives. Maybe he's just jovial by nature, but I have a theory that he was once a professional athlete and now he can't shake the habit. He is sunburned regardless of the season, and he has bleached streaks in his pushed-back hair, giving him a surfer vibe. I can't escape the notion that his entire youth unfolded on the crest of a wave in the North Sea, in front of all the vacationing girls, who swooned in a row at the water's edge. I truly believe that every person can learn to drive a car, he said the first time I sat behind his steering wheel, and it almost sounded like a magic spell. In the beginning my driving instructor was encouraging, and he respected my very evident fear of dying, which he said was normal when you get your license at a later age. When I stalled out at the railroad crossing, my heart pounding and honks coming from the cars behind us, he just smiled. Press the clutch, put it in first, and give me five, he said, sticking up his hand in my direction. When I'm stressed out I tend to hit his hand a little off-center, and the clapping sound is seldom optimal despite my best intentions. At a certain point, my driving instructor stopped telling me that my reactions were normal. Instead, he started saying that the world would be a boring place if everyone were exactly the same. Are you tired of me, I ask him as I turn the car off. My instructor can't deny this outright, but he tells me that it's refreshing that I'm not another eighteen-year-old, because after a while you get tired of hearing stories about going out clubbing and dumb parents. A lot of his younger students are also sullen and hard to talk to. I have many faults, but that's not something I can be accused of. My talking is far better than my driving, and I signal, turn, and accelerate to the sound of my own words. My instructor asks me how I felt about the drive myself. He takes out his little notepad and runs through various driving scenarios using primitive illustrations. Am I still a long way from the road test, I ask. Miles away, he says, and he takes out a calendar. In the beginning my instructor would tell me about particularly bad students of his who managed to get their licenses in the end. People from Somalia, for example, who had never learned to ride a bicycle. Then you're just lost when you get out into traffic, my instructor said, cycling experience is an absolute must. And then there was a seventy-eight-year-old widow who had been a passenger her entire life, and a mother of triplets from Lem. These stories gradually faded away as I myself became a cautionary tale. I started as a comic anecdote to be told over his dinner table, but in time I evolved into a tragic figure. I look at my driving instructor. He has dark circles under his eyes and has ceased to say that everyone can learn to drive a car. I sigh and hand him the keys. Neutral and emergency brake, he says, and flicks at the dice that hang in the rearview mirror.

MY SON HAS fallen asleep in the principal's arms. You need to get out a little, she says with a stern look, and I run up to the welcome party they're throwing at the højskole. The theme is Wild West, and pretty much everyone I can see has a checkered shirt on with a sheriff's star at their breast. Perhaps it's because I'm an only child that I'm always taken aback if I don't arouse applause wherever I go. On the other hand, I'm not sure what I had expected. The students are courteous and they ask me how it's going with the little one. They say that he's really cute, and that they've also got a little niece his age, or that they know someone who's recently become a mother. They remind me of how, when I visit my grandmother at the nursing home, I feign a burning interest in *Dancing with the Stars*. Who do you think will win this year, I yell into her hearing aid, and she looks back at me with a mild expression and shrugs her shoulders. I hide out in the bathroom to pass the time. Two students stumble into the neighboring stall and begin discussing my boyfriend in booming voices. He just doesn't give a fuck, one of them says, sounding deeply impressed, he is exactly who he is. They make a survey of his body, about which they are both enthusiastic, and I find myself nodding along in agreement. Now they've reached his head, which I recently shaved so his psoriasis could get some sun. He doesn't give a fuck, repeats the one student, if he wants to look like a skinhead then he'll look like a skinhead. They don't think my boyfriend is the type to go around attacking people, but in the face of injustice, they're pretty sure he would throw some punches. I wait a little while after they leave, and I go find my skinhead at the bar. Is it okay to drink while you're breastfeeding, one of the students asks, looking at my glass. My boyfriend gives me a green drink but then disappears into a sea of young hands. It's like tossing a steak to a litter of wild dogs. The students want him. Some want his body, others his attention. My boyfriend's earnestness is crystal clear and pure, and although that made navigating social life difficult for him out in the real world, here it's a triumph. The students' eyes are projectors, and my boyfriend smiles back in wonder, while I watch on, filled with a lonely pride.

WHEN MY BOYFRIEND gets home a little before midnight, I'm sitting on the sofa taking notes on Anders Agger's television programs. He's been to asylum centers, prisons, parliament, and autopsies, and he moves effortlessly between refugees, inmates serving life sentences, ministers of state, and corpses. Wherever he finds himself, people open up to him like wide French doors and lay their souls at his feet. My boyfriend hangs his cowboy hat on the bonsai tree and gets two beers out of the refrigerator. This time, Anders Agger is at Vestas, and he explains in a voiceover that the company's windmills were born out of classic West Jutlandic stubbornness after the oil crisis of the nineteen seventies. The technology was invented by a blacksmith who had a little surplus of iron and the idea that the wind was probably here to stay, Anders Agger says as the camera shows him in the middle of a whirring wind farm at sundown. He's understated, says my boyfriend, just like Columbo. Intelligent but harmless-seeming, a combination that's more rare than you'd think. I find a pen and start writing down keywords. The next episode takes us into a cloister of Jehovah's Witnesses in Tilst. We watch our favorite scene again and again. Anders Agger asks a male Witness how he feels about having indoctrinated his daughter, while the two of them are out proselytizing in a suburban neighborhood. It's cold, they're freezing, and no one wants to hear about Jehovah. The Witness is clearly offended and the vibe is about to get really bad, but then Anders Agger shivers, pours them both a paper cup of coffee, and says: Cheers. He establishes a bond, says my boyfriend, us against the weather, man against nature. Impressive, I say, and I take a swig of my beer. Cheers, the Witness says, already visibly relieved.

Dear Letterbox,

I recently got a new job at a small IT company. I like the work, and I feel confident in my ability to complete my tasks. However, I've been feeling a little insecure because the company works with a new operating system that I'm not at home with yet. Still, I have resisted asking my colleagues for help. My eldest daughter says I'm just being a stubborn camel, but I don't want to make the company regret hiring me. My wife thinks that I should feel safe about reaching out for help, but I'm not sure, and I'd rather stay up at night reading instruction manuals than lose face at work. What do you think I should do?

Sincerely,

The Stubborn Camel

Dear Stubborn Camel,

I think your wife is right that it's a good idea to talk to your colleagues regarding the operating system. Most people like to help others, and they find it especially pleasing when they actually know what they're talking about. This isn't supposed to be all about me, but let's take the example of my son's pediatric nurse, a very considerate person, who, for the record, I like. Having a child is a life crisis, she said to us sympathetically when she came for a home visit the day after I gave birth, and if you are unsure about anything you can always call me. I've taken her up on that offer many times, and regardless of what I ask, she will clear her throat and tell me that all children are different. In the beginning I would wait a moment, assuming that this was a sort of prelude, but over time I discovered that this was the introduction, explanation, and conclusion. The nurse ensured us that we as parents knew our son best, and that we were in the best position to find out what he needed. I stand in firm disagreement with this assessment, and I have to wonder why the vaunted wisdom of our medical authorities is so elusive when you actually need their help. I want commands and instruction manuals, instead of a little child who looks at me expectantly. At one point, big splotches began to develop on my son's skin under his arms and knees. My boyfriend and I stared at them. We discussed, considered, and guessed, while they spread out across his little body. Is it possible, the nurse asked us with infinite circumspection as she inspected our son, that perhaps you don't always get him completely clean. We looked at one another in panic. He was five weeks old. We had closely studied a diagram with images of baby poop at various phases of an infant's development. We had devoutly observed the state of his diapers. We had changed and powdered and oiled with such a passion that we had simply forgotten to wash him. Now he was about to mold away. All children are different, the nurse said, but perhaps try giving him a bath. Dear Stubborn Camel, nip this problem in the bud. Remember that all operating systems are different, and that the world is full of friendly people waiting in the wings to help us with life's challenges. Hold out your hand, and, sure enough, there will be someone there to give you a high five.

Sincerely,

The Letterbox

LOOKS LIKE IT'S Monday, I say, and I hang my son's jacket on a little coat hanger with a buttercup for a hook. There's no escaping it, says Maj-Britt. This week is all about farms, and they are studying which sounds go with which animals. On Friday they'll visit Nor's parents, who have a slaughterhouse in Herning. Moo, my son says. I think I win the mom trophy, I say, blowing a fanfare on an invisible trumpet, I made it here with his rainsuit and his indoor shoes today. Mom trophy, asks Maj-Britt. I think she actually does like me, but in a different way than she likes the other parents. More like I'm a helpless and slightly feebleminded asylum seeker who she needs to integrate into Danish society. You have holes in your stockings, says Ella, the oldest girl at the daycare. I can see your big toe, she says, and she grabs my foot. There's nothing wrong with that, says Maj-Britt, in fact it's the fashion some places in the world. What's fashion, asks Ella. It means it's cool, Maj-Britt says. A smell of strawberry mash wafts through the room. Can't you also look after me, I say, and I lay my jacket down on the bench in her kitchen. That would be *hyggelig*, Maj-Britt says, and she passes me a cup of coffee. She tells me that they're going on a treasure hunt down by the fjord today. I fantasize about how I could impress all the other kids by knowing the answers to the questions that would lead us to the treasure. For example, I can name all of the dwarves in *Snow White*. Sneezy, Sleepy, Happy, Bashful, Grumpy, Dopey, and Doc, I say, raising one finger in the air for each dwarf. Impressive, says Maj-Britt, and she wrings a bib out into the sink. It's a win-win, I say, no letters to answer, no editor talking about word counts. I could wear an adult-sized jumpsuit with Winnie the Pooh and Tigger on it. Maj-Britt nods. I could run around like a big baby and if I got sad you could hold me and rock me back and forth until everything was better. My son looks at Maj-Britt's whirring laundry machine and makes a loud, grunting sound. I could also just go to work, I say. Moo, says my son, and he waves at me. Something about his tone of voice makes it seem like a command.

KRISSER AND I are smoking outside the gym, and my pulse is hammering through my body. We may have rosy cheeks, but on the inside we're angry, because we've been working out and neither of us likes to exercise. Well that was that, Krisser says. That was that, I say. As a rule, our conversations consist of short sentences, and even though Krisser is one of the people I talk to most, I would never be able to summarize what we've talked about. When we drink leftover wine at the hotel, or beers down by the harbor, for the most part we just yell at each other, we roar with laughter like two farm animals who've just been let out to graze after a winter in the stable. You can smoke four a day when you're breastfeeding, Krisser says, but it's important to count them, because otherwise the baby won't ever develop resistance to bacteria. She heard this from a nurse who was totally down-to-earth. When Krisser talks about people, they always fall into one of three categories. The worst is *stressful*, then comes *totally down-to-earth*, and the best is *hyggelig*. I have an unhealthy desire to get into the last category. We're getting so thin, Krisser says. Buns of steel, I yell. I don't harbor any dreams of weight loss, but I want to be hyggelig, and if Krisser had said that we should swim with sharks or count every product in the supermarket, I'd have done it without blinking. As usual, I've forgotten a towel, but Krisser has started bringing two. I don't know what I'd do without you, I say, and I wipe the sweat off my face. Aw shucks, Krisser says, and she punches me on the shoulder. On the rare occasions that I say something sweet to Krisser, she always acts like I'm trying to tease her, even though I'm convinced that she can hear the difference. Shall we, Krisser says. Yes, let's, I say, and I get into her car. We drive slowly toward Velling, and we make a stop by the fjord where the geese are drawing big letters in the sky. They head south in slow Vs like a parade beneath the clouds, as if they were trying to impress us. Wow, I say. Exactly, answers Krisser, and we watch as countless flocks pass over the land of short sentences.

Dear Letterbox,

I am a thirty-seven-year-old man who is in treatment to deal with my long battle with alcohol abuse. I grew up in a troubled family, but I've finally broken free of the destructive patterns I learned in my childhood. My wife has supported me all the way, and I'm deeply grateful to her, but she can't really understand the demons that I'm struggling with. My mentor at AA is a middle-aged woman who knows exactly what I'm living through. My feelings for her have grown during the process, as have hers for me. I feel like she is my true soulmate rather than my wife, even though my wife has always stood by me. I'm confused and I feel so guilty.

Sincerely,

The Pattern Breaker

Dear Pattern Breaker,

Alas, soulmates rarely make for good couples, although I do understand the force of the attraction. Personally, I'm often drawn to people who are, like me, prone to losing control. Our restless spirits recognize each other across the room, and we feel the special bond that lies in the knowledge that we won't be alone when the time comes to lose ourselves in the music. But, dear Pattern Breaker, the sum of darkness that two people share must not be greater than the love, and this fact creates some very natural boundaries for who you can and cannot be with. When I fall in love with someone else's sorrow, and get swept into their craziness, I know I've got to get away as fast as possible. Trust me. It's best for everyone.

Kind regards,

The Letterbox

PEOPLE STOP AT the grocery store and make funny faces and strange noises to try to establish a connection with my son. They sidle up beside us and start talking right through him. What's your name, sweetie pie, what pretty curls you've got there. Are you out shopping with your mommy. Sometimes I answer them in a high, squeaky baby voice, and my son looks up at me in surprise, but as a rule I respond neutrally on his behalf like a professional ventriloquist. For the most part my son tolerates this, as if it's a part of the job, but sometimes he wrinkles his brow, puffs out his fat cheeks, and looks up in exasperation. I sympathize, it must be exhausting to be constantly spoken to like a cross between a house pet and a decorative object. The majority of these communiqués digress into anecdotes about the observer's own children or grandchildren, their neighbor's baby daughter, or a nephew who's also about to turn one. Elderly people smile at me, they smile at their own younger selves, they smile at their spouses, who float invisibly in the air behind me. Adolescent girls light up, filled with vague intuitions of a distant future, which momentarily manifests in the form of my son's face. Middle-aged men with half-grown sons who soon won't be able to be referred to as children any longer are struck with the sudden longing for a little body that you can throw up in the air and catch again to the entirely predictable sound of laughter. These are the sorts of dreams and memories that flow toward us, and I understand that, for the first time in my life, I've become someone who other people identify with. That a child is never just itself, but all children who have been and will be. That motherhood is not one's own, but a thousand people's motherhoods. Suddenly I see Anders Agger behind a shopping cart slowly rolling between the candles and the napkins. I follow him at a distance of thirty feet, allowing other customers to come between us, along with the occasional grocer walking with quick steps toward the stockroom. When Anders Agger stops, as if in thought, and sets something down into his cart, I stop too. I stand still and contemplate the pumpkin I've picked up, shifting my gaze between it and Anders Agger. I'm dying to see his communication skills in action, to witness in the flesh what I imagine would be a one hundred percent successful conversation. Judging by what I can make out from behind a column by the freezers, his purchases appear to be politically correct. I head for the produce section and grab a bag of organic oranges. Anders Agger picks up a head of cabbage and considers its purple leaves. Then he gently sets it down with his other products. I wonder if he's the type who pickles them himself, or if he sautés them in butter and sea salt. When he goes up to one of the employees and asks where the pomegranates are, it dawns on me that he might even eat it raw. Finely sliced, mixed with oranges and chopped walnuts. A woman pokes Anders Agger on the shoulder and tells him that he has revitalized the documentary as a genre. He looks happy to hear that, even though he tells her that it's an exaggeration. You make us everyday people feel seen, she says. I search Anders Agger's face for a trace of weariness, but I find none. He asks the woman about her life, and she tells him that she's a preschool teacher, but back in her day she actually dreamed of being a pilot. It might be something for one of your programs, she says with a cackle. A family with children and a little cart carrying tasting samples get between us and I can't see how Anders Agger extricates himself from the conversation. As I walk past the ecstatically smiling preschool-pilot lady, she's typing out a text message, her fingers dancing in haste. At the registers, Anders Agger chooses the line next to mine, and he stares at the contents of my shopping cart. With the exception of a frozen pizza, it's exactly identical to his selection. He looks up at me, a little alarmed, and puts a pack of cream puffs next to the future cabbage salad. Looks like it's Friday, I say, trying my best to sound cheerful. Anders Agger nods and says that there's no escaping it. My son has been hypnotized by the rolling conveyor belt and is of no help at all. I just love making cabbage salad from scratch, I say loudly to the cashier, and I hum as I put the products into my bag. Well, good luck with the cabbage, Anders Agger says when he walks by me with his bags. Back at you, I say, time to get chopping. Anders Agger waves as he glides by and turns onto Herningvej, and I just manage to memorize his license plate number.

MOO, SAYS MY son, as though he's just made a decision about something. The tones of his moos rise and fall, and are capable of expressing an array of complex feelings. I wake in the morning to the sound of a high-pitched voice mooing from inside the nursery, and I think of it as a prelude to the day. My life is a symphony of cow sounds, and they follow me wherever I go. Moohooo, yells my son, enraptured, as he points to a windmill. Moo, he whispers perplexedly when the højskole students ask him his name in the cafeteria. The principal picks up my son and carries him over to look at the statue. Grundtvig, she says, pointing up at it. Moo, my son says seriously, reaching out for its stone nose. Now he wants to play with the immersion blender, with that beautiful spinning metal that glints in the light of the kitchen lamp. No, I say. Moohooo, he screams, like one possessed, like a crazed bull in heat. He crawls toward me, his head bowed, charging at the air, and then he points at the blender before hurling himself to the floor. His cries escalate in tempo and volume. Moomoomoo, he gasps, tears running down his cheeks, moomooooooooo. At the fence along the roadside his hands begin to flap in the air, his legs move like little drumsticks, and he points and smiles. He wants to crawl around between the cows' legs, to gently tug on their tails, to feed them grass and dandelions, to feel their rough tongues on his hands. He wants to sing in their choir, to bellow out over the fields, the call of ten thousand cows breaking against the waves of the North Sea. He needs to move along in the alphabet, says my boyfriend, who has read a book about speech training. We try everything. Dogs, cats, mice, frogs, owls, lions, bears. We agree to focus on one animal at a time. What does the sheep say, my boyfriend asks slowly. Moo, says our son, and he looks at us like we're falling behind in school. We discover a flock of sheep in a meadow outside of Stauning, and we spend a couple of weekends out there. We pack a picnic and walk back and forth with the fold. We buy expensive, extra-soft toilet paper printed with lambs, and a big, fluffy stuffed sheep. Baaa, we say, gently, encouragingly. My son furrows his brow, looking like he'll never forgive us for anything when he lies down one day on the sofa in the psychologist's office and reflects on his childhood. Moo, he says, and rolls his eyes.

Dear Letterbox,

I'm a male high school teacher. I've only recently finished my education and gotten my first real job. I started school early and have gone right through without any breaks, so I'm only twenty-five years old, which means I'm actually pretty close to the students, age-wise. I get a lot of comments from them on my looks, especially after they've had a few beers in the cafeteria on Friday afternoons, and it can be really awkward. I used to be a model, and I take pride in my appearance, but do you think I should take some kinds of precautions in this situation? I'm an advisor for a group of the older students, and one of them tends to hit on me after she's had a couple drinks. She's cute and smart, but I shouldn't go there, right?

Sincerely,

The Advisor

Dear Advisor,

It's a shame when good looks create a stumbling block in one's professional life. When I was really pregnant, I had a teacher at my driving school called Mona. The problem with Mona was painfully obvious. She was simply too sexy to be a teacher at a driving school. I wasn't alone in this struggle. The sweaty, teenage boys in my class couldn't focus on her overhead projections either. She spoke with such a strong Jutlandic dialect that it made my Aarhusian accent sound almost like that of a Copenhagener, which is saying something. When she went through the traffic laws, we would sit there drooling, trying to impress her with our knowledge of the rules of right-of-way. Mona's hair was almost orange, and though I don't actually care for the color, I became addicted to it. It always complemented her clothes in some nuanced way, and it wouldn't be an exaggeration to say that she was radiant. Mona was Pippi Longstocking on her horse, a big bouquet of orange dahlias, and her smile was a hazard light flashing in the night. The students at the driving school sat breathlessly beside Mona in her BMW while she ate hard candies and read the funny text messages her friends would send her aloud. I was in my ninth month of pregnancy and my driving skills were still hopeless. My road test kept getting pushed back, as if it were trying to land on my due date. Listen here, preggo, Mona yelled as she saw me waddling toward her with my huge belly, if you give birth in my car you've gotta clean it yourself, and she opened the door for me. Dear Advisor, it may seem like there are unexpected opportunities to be found in these flat plains, and the horizon can seem impossibly distant. It's not. Keep your eyes on the road. A BMW is not a delivery room, and a classroom is not a nightclub. You don't hook up with your students, and you don't give birth in other people's cars.

Warm regards,

The Letterbox

I STEP OUT of the train station in Skjern. The houses look flat through the drizzle. Look, I say, pointing to a bizarre building. It resembles a work of postmodern art from the late eighties, and I feel like I've been smoking weed. The main building is a color somewhere between a sun-bleached yellow and a faded beige, and the wings on either side are incongruous and modern, suitable for housing municipal offices and stressed-out caseworkers. A strange tower rises toward the clouds above the main building, but is weighed down by a brown awning that looks like the canopy of a baby carriage. Two symmetrical portholes adorn each side of it like eyes, and they study the train station as if standing guard over the town's visitors. The confusion of styles is total, and I imagine that it was drawn up by a drunken architect, who was later replaced by a new team of architects, equally drunk but with different ideas. The work is crowned by a tall spire that disappears into the sky. I'm speechless, I say to my son, who sprinkles me with drool. Krisser comes rushing out of the building's swinging doors with Vera in her arms. We go inside and sit down at the restaurant. A pair of identical twins whisper to one another by the kitchen door. This is Pia and this is Maria, Krisser says, pointing at one and then the other. It's the other way around, one of them says. We're in the same mothers' group, Krisser says, now pointing at me. The twins say hello in unison, and a smile glides across both of their faces like a passing train. I thought we were friends, I say to Krisser when we sit down. Aw shucks, she says, hitting me in the arm, we can be both. After we've been sitting for a few minutes, Krisser waves the twins over. As if in slow motion, Pia and Maria pick up one menu each and amble in the direction of our table. I order a Fanta, but Krisser gets a sparkling water. Citrus flavored or unflavored, Pia asks, her eyes on her notepad. You sound like you're asking me whether I'd prefer to be buried or cremated, Krisser says, is life really so bad. The twins look at one another and shake their heads. Good workers don't exactly grow on trees around here, Krisser says once Pia and Maria have gone back to the bar. One of them holds out the glass while the other presses the button that gets water to spray out of the machine. When Krisser bought Hotel Skjern, it was as much a statement as an entrepreneurial dream. Her plan grew and grew, and when she sat down at the bank with stars in her eyes, the financial advisors were struck with a sudden desire to loan her a ton of money. After that, everybody wanted to hop onto her magic carpet. When she hired her chef, he handed her a long and impressive résumé, but she batted it away. I want you to do your very best, she said, and make me a caffe latte without burning the milk. Right away, he answered, looking into her eyes, and like everyone else who beholds Krisser, he wanted to please her. People have an instinctive drive to ensure Krisser's happiness, because it's easiest for everyone, but also because it doesn't take long to love her. She whirled through the kitchen issuing orders to her employees. She had a way of getting them to sound like compliments, and they always answered: Yes, Krisser, of course. After they added an extra floor onto the hotel, guests came streaming in from all over Jutland, and Krisser showed them the local sights all summer long. She organized trips to Skjern Meadows and took them on barge outings through the wetlands. It was while he was fording this river in 1513 that King Hans was thrown from his horse, Krisser explained, and he died soon after in what was Danish history's deadliest case of pneumonia. *Was gefallt*, the German tourists asked her, taking photographs of an old watchtower. *Pferd, Fluss, tot*, Krisser answered, *gross König*. When Krisser pointed out an osprey, they looked up to the sky and nodded, as if she herself had discovered the bird and placed it in the air. When she was nine months pregnant, she waddled around placing orders for art for the new rooms. You're tormenting me with all these happy colors, Krisser cried out, and she still claims that it was Poul Pava who induced her labor. *WE'RE ALL JUST BIG CHILDREN* it said in big, round, cartoonish letters on a Pava painting her husband had hung in the bridal suite. Beside the text, a crazed-looking stick figure smiled at the viewer. Karsten, Krisser screamed, the party's over. By the time her husband got there her water had already broken. What's wrong with the Skagen Painters, she screamed, Krøyer, Ancher, Tuxen, there are so many possibilities. Call Theis, Krisser gasped, and her husband grabbed his phone. He began desperately ordering framed prints, and Vera came into the world in room 211 just twenty minutes later. Right under Poul Pava, says Krisser, smiling down at her daughter.

CAN YOU BELIEVE we're picking mushrooms, I said, I've never done this before. Foraging, Sebastian says, one forages for mushrooms. We walk through the school's organic gardens and stare down at the ground while flocks of birds glide slowly across the sky. Button mushrooms, chanterelles, yellowfoot mushrooms, Sebastian mumbles. Our children are sitting under a fir tree and smearing dirt on one another's faces. For Sebastian, it's been a revelation to move to the countryside, and he's recently been thinking about becoming totally self-sufficient. You can actually make the vast majority of household products yourself, he says, it's only a lack of imagination that holds people back. Toothpaste, shampoo, toilet paper, I say. Sebastian waves my skepticism away. His smile is open and diffuse, as if it's not directed at a specific person but at the world itself. You're a composer, I say, you don't know anything about agriculture. Sebastian tells me that we all bear a knowledge of nature deep within us, and the rest we can read up on. We sit down on two tree stumps, and I take a bite of a beautiful mushroom that I've just plucked from the ground. Don't chew, Sebastian shouts. He hits me between the shoulder blades while sticking his fingers into my mouth. That's a destroying angel, he yells, it can make you go deaf and blind. I'm still spitting into the soil when Sebastian's eldest daughter comes running over. Do you want to watch my dance show, she asks, jabbing her finger into my shoulder. It's impossible to take the question as anything but a threat. We walk over to their house, and Alba pulls on a neon-green tutu and points to the sofa, where we are to sit. Sebastian looks tired as he hands me a glass of kombucha. No thanks, I say, that looks like morning pee. Microphone, Alba yells, and her little sister crawls under the table to retrieve a hairbrush. I love Sebastian's children, because they're growing up before my eyes. Because they pee in the same kiddie pool as my son, and they grow, smile, and develop in the same uneven rhythm. Uuuunder the starry skyyyyy, Alba sings as loudly as she can while she spins around and around. I feel dizzy, and Sebastian's eyes look empty as he watches his daughter. When I was pregnant, people told me that you make new friends after you have children but I rejected the notion categorically because it sounded like such a conventional way of thinking. Before I became a mother myself, I couldn't have imagined the power of parenthood, but it's actually not so different from the other hobbies we pursue, maniacal, inspired, and unworthy, throughout our lives. When you have children, you gain access to a club, just like being a smoker. You leave the party together, step out into the cold, stand a little more closely than you need to. You look at one another knowingly right before you light up, and you understand exactly how the other person is feeling. Social class, political opinions, age, and gender dissolve into a shared passion which everyone knows will make you tired, ugly, and old before your time. You know it's unforgivably stupid, yet you can't possibly live without it, and you're always wondering when you'll have your next one. This shared experience becomes an alliance, born of a wild and boundless love, which earlier in life you had directed toward sports heroes or pop stars. It's over now, Alba yells, you have to clap.

Song for a Windless Autumn
Birthday Song

Melody: Sleep Tight, Little Child
(Sov sødt, barnlille)
Composer: Thomas Laub, 1915

1 The flag is waving
the horses are neighing
because they've been told
you've turned one year old
so silently sleeping as night falls
my autumn child
in dreamland's wilds
you are so dizzyingly small.

2 A cow left the field
to a ship did steal
and without a word
he climbed right aboard
to survey the endless sea
like that cow you moo
your bovine tune
a calf has been born to me.

3 The sunlight descends
   into the playpen
   and before my eyes
   you grow in size
   I can speak of you endlessly
   but what I mean
   is I love everything
   you are, have been, and will be.

4 We watch cows and sheep
   minutes turn to weeks
   and as nature planned
   you expand and expand
   like rings in the trunk of a tree
   your will is free
   you rage blindly
   a cascade of tears and pee.

5 My love has no fear
   peace always is near
   love makes no demands
   every challenge withstands
   always is prepared for tomorrow
   for parents know grace
   can come in a place
   that is not unlike fear and sorrow.

6 The flag is waving
   the windmills gyrating
   this happy commotion
   is made in devotion
   to you on your very first birthday
   I wish you, my dear
   a wonderful year
   and bright memories to hold always.

THE DRIVING SCHOOL instructors have their own little fiefdom in the form of a bar and grill between Videbæk, Spjald, and Ringkøbing. See you at The Main Office, they shout when they pass one another in traffic, lifting imaginary hot dogs to their mouths, and they meet up in the evening as soon as the last student steps out of their cars. They are rolling detectives, they know every shop and every street, down to the littlest flower. They keep an eye out for roadwork and places with temporarily reduced speed limits. Nothing escapes the keen gaze of the driving instructors. This little mafia is sitting at The Main Office, exchanging news from the public sphere, and on the table sit all manner of variations on the hot dog, some piled with roasted onions, others fully enveloped by the bun, some sausages wrapped up in bacon, and plain frankfurters with the bun on the side. My driving teacher has invited me along and he buys me a pork sandwich. We sit down at the table, and he takes a deep breath. It's not that I don't like you, he begins, this isn't about you, it's about me. My driving instructor scratches his head and mumbles something about how he just needs a change. We keep no secrets here, Parking Peter says to me, so you need to know that you'll be switching driving instructors. Harlot, Mona says, and takes a bite of her hot dog. I can feel a little piece of cabbage stuck to my face, and the surfer hands me a napkin. Mona lost, he says, passing her the timetable where my practice hours are recorded, but I believe you two know each other already. I wipe my mouth. You're sure taking your time with this, little mama, Mona says as she picks up her keys. We go out to her BMW and smoke a cigarette. Sometimes we draw straws for the students after we get off, she says, the ones who can't cut it, I mean. Students who take longer to reach proficiency guarantee a certain income, of course, but they can also wear you down. Just to tell it like it is, she says. The driving instructors have passed me off to one another in a desperate relay ever since I passed the written test. In the beginning it always goes well. Before long I know the names of all of their family members and pets. I hear about their upbringing here in the province, their school years and marriages, affairs and childhood memories. The driving instructors become a novel, and I always look forward to the day's chapter. I soon forget that it's a driving school at all, traffic becomes a strange pretense, and the lessons continue. Then they start to look askance at me and their tempers grow shorter. I destroy the psyches of my driving instructors. I wound their professional pride every single time I sit down in their cars. In the end, my very presence represents defeat, forces them to ask whether they've landed in the right job. Uncertainty batters them down, blankets their entire being. Is this the right marriage, the right children, the right life. Once you begin to doubt things, the thoughts spread like ripples through the water. In the end, no one can take it. I'm seeing a pattern here, Mona says, and it hits me that I'm being fired by the people I myself have hired. She tells me that the surfer has had to take time off to deal with his stress, that he's a control freak and can't cope with failure. By which you mean me, I say, and she nods. But he's always been a little, she says, and I feel a grammatical malaise, because she rarely finishes her sentences. A little what, I say. A little you know, Mona says, and she taps her temple with her index finger. She smiles to me with her gray bedroom eyes, which go so well with her golden sneakers. Remember to let the clutch up slowly, Mona says right before the car stalls out. Slowly, she repeats, now give it a little gas. She rolls up the sleeves of her cardigan and reveals two forearms that resemble the tunnel in Vejlby-Risskov I used to bike through on the way to school. Her tattoos depict cats from various angles, with strange smiles and simple stripes. They have bows in their hair, they jump around and eat cupcakes, they wear superhero capes and top hats. Hello Kitty, I say. Yep, says Mona. She turns on the radio, and I ask how things are going with her. Depends how you look at it, she says, and she opens a pack of nicotine gum with violent motions. Look at what, I ask. Life, she says. She's cutting back on smoking, and she admits that she's not in the best of moods. Back inside The Main Office, the surfer raises his hand. Whether he's waving or giving me an air high five is difficult to tell, but I can see that the color has returned to his cheeks.

MY BOYFRIEND AND I are at the annual town festival at Velling's athletic fields. The Velling Resident of the Year is going to be elected, and I write down the principal's name in capital letters and draw a heart around it. The grocer is sitting with two other men in a cage in the middle of the field. What's this about, I ask, sticking my finger between the bars. We're raising money for a new arena, he says, an addition to the charter school, but everyone in the community will be able to use it. It'll be Velling's answer to Boxen in Herning, the grocer says, and he tells me how it was Dorthe who originally sat in the cage. What did she do to deserve that, I ask. She's a mother of three, says the grocer, and the idea was that she wouldn't get let out of the cage until they raised more than five hundred thousand kroner. Dorthe's children came and stuck drawings through the bars, and one night you could even hear her singing goodnight songs for her youngest, who was standing outside the cage with his teddy bear. It made an impression, says the grocer. The farmers put their heads together, the højskole's board held an emergency meeting, and even Foot & Face chipped in. In the end they got three hundred thousand together, and Dorthe came out of the cage only on the condition that the festival committee get locked up in her place. The three men drink their beers and laugh. From damsel in distress to lion's den, says the grocer. Krisser is sitting with her husband beside the beer keg. Velling's priest is griping about the prices at the cafés in Ringkøbing, thirty-five kroner for a half liter of sparkling water. I can see Krisser's pupils slowly turning red. The priest says he can get a liter and a half of sparkling water at the grocery store for only eight kroner. Karsten is always warning Krisser about this, that she shouldn't talk about the hotel when she's been drinking. Do you want to sit in the grocery store and drink sparkling water, Krisser asks. Between the aisles, she pauses, or perhaps in the frozen section. No, says the priest, looking confused. Krisser raises her eyebrows in feigned amazement. Okay then, she says slowly, so you'd rather sit in a rattan chair on the square, in the sunshine, perhaps. The priest nods and ties his gray hair back into a ponytail. And would you like to drink this sparkling water from a glass, perhaps even with a slice of lemon, does that sound nice, Krisser says softly. Yes, mumbles the priest, looking around for his congregation. Krisser smiles in a way that sends a shiver down my spine. You don't get the glass yourself from the café's kitchen, do you, whispers Krisser. What did you say, the priest asks, sliding closer to her. I'm saying that things cost money, Krisser screams, that nothing in this world is free. Karsten cautiously pats her back. Suddenly the mayor arrives with a big envelope under his arm. The principal hooks up the microphone and follows him up onto the stage. Repeat after me, thunders Krisser: rent, salaries, inventory. The mayor clears his throat and says he has some good news for Velling. He follows this remark with a lengthy, theatrical pause, of the sort that only middle-aged men attempt. He's about to reveal the results of the collection, and he airs the possibility that the three men will soon be able to come out of the cage. People beat their fingers on their tables in a communal drumroll. Insurance, advertising, income tax, I can hear the priest repeating to my right. It looks like we've been able, in just two weeks, to collect eight hundred thousand kroner for the new arena. Sales tax, Krisser yells, and people leap to their feet in applause. The atmosphere is euphoric. The cage is opened, and the three men come out and stand up on the stage with their arms around one another's shoulders. The ovation is endless, and the men bow and bow. The autumn twilight wraps itself around the tent, and Velling surrounds us like a mythological landscape. We drink our keg beers and we dance the hokeypokey, and that's what it's all about. The principal stands on the bar with a microphone in her hand. Sing, she yells, sing so they can hear you all the way to Ringkøbing. We're from Velling, we're from Velling, olé, olé, olé, we bellow across the fjord, which answers us with its lingering sigh.

Dear Letterbox,

I'm the type of person who thinks a lot about others, as opposed to my husband, who falls into the group of people who think mostly about themselves. We often get into fights about our different values, and we disagree about how we are going to raise our children. What can I do to get him to change?

Sincerely,

The Thoughtful One

Dear Martyr,

You know the type of person who is always saying what type of person they are. They are never the type that they think. When people define themselves, they are in fact revealing their greatest wishes or their deepest fear. You can never trust an institution that investigates itself, police officers who are questioned by their friends, or academics who quote their own articles. Speak kindly of your husband, dear Martyr, we all have a responsibility when a fellow motorist needs to merge into our lane. Just because you can't see yourself, it doesn't mean that you are invisible.

Sincerely,

The Letterbox

WHO PISSED ON your dessert, Bent asks me as I pass him on the way into the daycare with my son under my arm. I explain that I live at a højskole, that I risk permanent brain damage from being surrounded by excessively happy people. My negativity is instinctive, I say, it's about maintaining the balance of the cosmos. When all of the students get together, they're like an army on the march to war. Armed with peace and love, there's no stopping them. Wouldn't that wear you out, I ask. Sure would, Bent says, waving to my son as he grabs his scarf. In theory, I believe in community and all those beautiful values, I say, sitting down on the kitchen bench, but they seem to have deserted me. Moo, says my son, and he reaches his arms out for his daycare teacher. Maj-Britt has baked green buns, and she sets two halves down in front of me on a plate. Wow, I say, and I take a bite. She puts food coloring in the dough because the kids think it's fun. Just to shake things up around here, Maj-Britt says. She tells me that my son's outdoor suit is about to fall apart as she brushes an egg wash onto a blue baguette. Every time I step into the daycare I get the feeling of having forgotten my script. Say something normal, I think, something neutral. Maj-Britt tells me that they are doing gymnastics later today. Wall bars, I think, balance beams, climbing walls, dodgeball. I claimed that I started menstruating when I was ten years old, I say, so I could get out of gymnastics classes, and I pour coffee into the cup in front of me. Interesting, says Maj-Britt, as she puts a baking pan into the oven. I actually got my period for the first time when I was twelve, I continue, but gymnastics teachers can't really verify that sort of thing. Now my words are unstoppable. They go on and on like a street fight from which you can't extricate yourself. My lips rattle up and down like a sewing machine, and my thoughts transform directly into words with no sign of redaction. My brain attempts to send SOS signals to my larynx, the warm hearth of my affliction. It forwards the messages on to my vocal chords, which sling themselves gleefully across my trachea. When none of these obey, it summons my nose and sinus cavities in a panic. It's incredible how bad my body is at teamwork. It must be the same with people who are repeatedly unfaithful, maybe they just can't control their sexual organs. But on that front I'm actually very disciplined, I say to Maj-Britt. As soon as I feel the pangs of lust flowing through my body, I shut my eyes and call a cab. A taxi, three cheeseburgers, and straight to bed. Sounds like a flawless method of contraception, Maj-Britt says.

THE PRINCIPAL AND I are going to Foot & Face in Velling. She's having foot, but I'm opting for face, because I can't stand people touching my feet. I got a gift card from the owner when we moved in, along with a potted plant. The card is good for a foot, which is cheaper than face, but I'll do anything to avoid foot. Does it seem ungrateful to upgrade to face, I ask the principal. I don't think foot is quite what you're imagining, says the principal, who has been going there for many years. Did you tell them you were coming with a friend when you booked the appointment, I ask her as we cross the train tracks. No, says the principal, I said that I was coming with my neighbor. But do you think of us as friends, I ask. Neighbors are vital when you live in the countryside, she says. The principal starts to tell a story about Theis and his wife, whose contractions started in the middle of the night while their car was being repaired. Cabbie-Connie was away on vacation and her substitute driver had been called all the way out to Bur, so the only one left to drive them was the neighbor. Theis's wife ended up giving birth in their neighbor's Skoda, says the principal, right in front of the bar and grill on Brejningvej. And the second time, it happened exactly the same, except in their own car. The third time, they almost made it to the hospital, but by then Theis had perfected his delivery technique. At the bank where he worked they started calling him The Midwife. People yell, Call Theis, whenever someone's water breaks in Velling. It's become a sort of shorthand, says the principal, who often deploys local lore to escape from awkward situations. I really thought we were friends, I say. I think we will be, she says, all signs are good, and she takes me by the arm.

Dear Letterbox,

I am a young woman and I'll be graduating from secondary school next year. Both of my parents have top jobs at Vestas, but I want to go in a totally different direction and study the history of ideas. When I try to tell them about the philosophers I've been reading, my mom and dad get tired looks on their faces, and they try to turn the conversation back to wind energy as quickly as possible. It's like we're living in different worlds and we can't get through to one another. We fight a lot about politics and our different values, and I'm considering cutting all contact with them after I move to Copenhagen, or maybe seeing them only at Christmas. Do you think that's the right thing to do?

Best wishes,

The Black Sheep of the Family

Dear Black Sheep,

Let's get something straight: it is entirely possible to love people who you don't in fact even like, and this phenomenon is often observed among close family members. We are all born into a story that we haven't asked to be a part of, and our lives begin with a brutal decision that was made without our consent. The bond of blood isn't a red ribbon adorning our hair, it's a worn-out jump rope, an umbilical cord that binds us by the hands and feet. Familial sorrows rarely get better with time, because we can never really let go of hope, and there's always one last I forgive you left in our hearts. When you love someone with the blindness of instinct, what they do is almost inconsequential, what matters is who they are. Sweet Black Sheep, I know that it's of no comfort, but try to think of love as a confused moth, a hopeless, winged dance in the flames of a votive candle. The fire may singe it, a sudden breeze may dim the flame, but before long the moth will dance back toward the light, again and again, and it will never stop.

Warm regards,

The Letterbox

I SEE ANDERS Agger's car outside the library, and I park my bicycle beside it. I reserved a book about costume design, I say to the librarian, who shakes her head apologetically when she can't find my name in her files. Anders Agger is walking through the aisles of the non-fiction section, and I speculate that he's finding books for his research. I don't understand, I say, and I start talking about skeleton costumes. He stops and looks out the window. The fjord lies beautifully before him, as if it were trying to impress, as if it existed for him alone. The librarian looks at her screen one more time. Looks like it's Halloween, I say when I catch Anders Agger's eye. He nods, and the librarian intently scrutinizes a stack of books lying on a cart. Anders Agger goes down to the *K*s, close to the kids' corner. Do you want to go play, I say loudly to my son, who has fallen asleep in my arms. He might be a bit on the young side, says the librarian, but I'm already heading in the direction of a giant abacus. I pick up a copy of *Ronia, the Robber's Daughter* and start reading it out loud when my phone vibrates. Before I can say hello I have to sneeze. You're always getting sick, my mother says on the other end of the line. No, I say, like every average Dane I'm sick three point five times per year. My mother hasn't been sick in twenty years. I remind her about the kidney stones in 2005. My mom says you can't really call that a sickness, because anybody can get those. She thinks it's a pity that I've inherited my father's low pain threshold as well as his poor immune system. Two undesirable traits that reinforce one another, my mother says. She contends that when you add it all up, she spent half of their relationship in the pharmacy and the rest of the time in the hospital. It was almost as just hard for me as for him, she says, because I'm so empathetic. I had to bear witness to your father's monthly near-death experiences, each one brought on by the common cold. My mother's pain threshold is very high, and she starts to tell me about when I was born. It was just like peeling an almond, says my mother. My father usually clears his throat when he hears this. Almond after almond, he says. Your father's so sensitive, they practically had to carry him out of the delivery room, my mother says. He was outside smoking, I say. Cigarette after cigarette, my mother says.

I ATTEND THE same driving school as Malte, a student in my boyfriend's writing course, and once in a while we go on practice drives together. Malte has fallen painfully in love with Mona, and she's become the subject of most of his poems, though he transposes her onto other people and objects. We sit in the principal's steel-green Toyota and practice driving straight ahead on a gravel road. Two horses lift their heads and stop chewing as I drive by the stud farm. Eyes on the road, Malte says, and I put it into second gear. He takes his phone out of his pocket and smiles. He stares covetously at the "like" that Mona has placed under a photo of a Tesla. I ask Malte what he did over the weekend, and he tells me that he got a ticket for spraying graffiti on some old, abandoned warehouses. A little graffiti never hurt anybody, I say, as long as you make your tags good and avoid corny platitudes. Malte says that he mostly does quotations from poems and drawings of animals. I myself spent a few years riding my bike around and spraying *carpe diem* in the tunnels of Aarhus, I say, that sort of thing is uncalled for. Malte wants to be an artist, but he says that taking over his father's architecture business is probably what's in the cards for him. The two aren't mutually exclusive, I say, most of the members of Pink Floyd were architecture students, and they met each other in the middle of a town-planning session. What's Pink Floyd, asks Malte. I hit the turn signal, pull over, open the glove compartment, and put a CD in. *Wish You Were Here* is a good place to start, I say. I feel my father moving within me, and the twelve years separating Malte and me are like a

Berlin Wall between us. Shine On You Crazy Diamond, I say, shut your eyes and feel the music. Malte looks furtively at his phone. I'll just borrow this a moment, I say, and I throw it in the back seat. Listen to the lyrics, I say as I turn it up. But there's no singing, Malte says, yawning. Though the intro lasts eight and a half minutes, I tell him he's being impatient. Listen how the music expands, I say, and I promise to send him some links. Malte reaches around to the back seat and finds his phone. Okay, he mumbles as he opens the door. Don't you mean thank you, I say.

Dear Letterbox,

I'm a middle-aged man, who, after a particularly difficult period at work, has been diagnosed with acute stress disorder. Now I sit in my garden and stare at the grass all day. I can see that it's grown a little more each morning, but I can't bring myself to cut it. I've been with my current girlfriend for eight months. She is very caring and gives me the space I need, but I feel a lot of guilt. When we met, I was strong and energetic, but right now even a trip to the grocery store feels like an impossible endeavor. I don't think she'd do it herself, so maybe I should leave my girlfriend for her own sake, and follow Sting's instructions: If You Love Somebody, Set Them Free.

Sincerely,

The Troubled One

Dear Troubled One,

Like many others, I enjoy standing at the railing when I'm out on a boat. I've noticed that most people who look down into the churning sea hold tightly to the railing, as if something could suck them down. I think that there are two types of people on the ships of the night of the night. Those who are afraid they will fall, and those who are afraid they will jump. If there's one thing that makes me paranoid, it's other people's trust in me. I have an urge to betray them as quickly as possible, just to get it over with. When my boyfriend fell in love with me ten years ago, I felt a pang of sympathy for him. I saw his beaming eyes and I thought: You're going to regret this. Big time. His love is careless and unguarded, and even when I'm acting crazy, he looks at me like someone who refuses to abandon hope despite standing in the direct path of an impending natural disaster. Dear Troubled One, don't listen to Sting, for he merely offers the path of least resistance. The most important duty in a relationship is to restrain your own self-hatred. One blessing in the love of a partner is that they receive our sorrows like small gifts. Thank you, they say, and they carry them along as if the darkness were their own. Life is so beautiful that way.

Warm regards,

The Letterbox

THERE'S A SPECIAL dinner at the school tonight, and the theme is climate change. Inflatable globes have been fastened to all the lamps, and the students are dressed in outfits they have sewed together out of trash bags. The appetizer is roasted wood ants with steamed spinach. The organic nutrition teacher tells us that she's spent the whole week catching them in a coniferous forest outside of Tarm. The rest of the ingredients have been assembled from trash containers behind big supermarkets by students from the green entrepreneurship course. You should never trust the expiration date, says the organic nutrition teacher vehemently, the amount of perfectly good food that gets thrown away is simply barbaric. She says that, in her household, dumpster diving determines the dinner menu, and that we've got to liberate ourselves from our preconceived notions about cooking. The students have scavenged eighty-four pounds of brown sugar, and now it's just a question of creative thinking, says the organic nutrition teacher, limitations only reveal a poor imagination. Suddenly she looks startled, and she points to our son. Don't you ever clip his nails, she asks, in a voice quavering in shock and disbelief. Of course, my boyfriend and I say in unison. Without taking her eyes off us, the organic nutrition teacher calls out for her husband. She whispers something to him, and he shoots us a quick look. Five minutes later, he returns with the little nail clipper that they use on their youngest. He's out of breath, and he passes the nail clipper to his wife. She carefully removes my son's bib while she sings a children's song I've never heard before. My son sits completely still, his eyes wide open as his nails fall to the table. The organic nutrition teacher's husband stares intently at the whites of our son's eyes. They can easily scratch their pupils if their nails aren't regularly clipped, he whispers. You can look away for just a moment and suddenly they're either blind or permanently visually impaired. And do you happen to be an eye doctor, I say, as I gather the little nails together in a napkin. I do indeed, says the organic nutrition teacher's husband. He tells us that he has a clinic in Ringkøbing, right by the main square, specializing in glaucoma and cataracts. Well, maybe you should report us to the local authorities, I say. The organic nutrition teacher and her husband exchange a look, but they quickly shake their heads. The eye doctor looks at us earnestly and says that all parents do the best they can, and that it never helps to beat yourself up. As long as you're open and willing to learn along the way, there's nothing else to it, says the organic nutrition teacher. After the meal, a group of students has organized an activity they call Confessions. For the past few weeks there's been a heart-shaped paper box sitting outside of the dining hall, into which students could drop notes telling their secrets, and now Emma is reading them aloud. One of the secrets is that a student wants to hook up with my boyfriend on the school trip. Emma blushes, but she stares at my boyfriend as if she'd made him a proposition. Do I look invisible, I whisper to Sebastian. He shakes his head, and I stand up. I loudly clear my throat and try to catch Emma's eye. At first, laughter spreads, but when I keep on doing it, silence falls over the room. Can't you just send him dead animals or used menstrual pads like a normal stalker, I say, pointing at Emma, this has all gotten way too complicated. She bats her eyes at me, and the room is completely still. It's just for fun, Emma mumbles, don't you have a sense of humor. No, I say, I'm running low on humor at the moment. You're a bunch of confused, horny children, and you have no idea about real life. Yes we do, says Emma. My boyfriend stares at a painting of a tango dancer as if the two of them were the only people on earth. It's good to get it out, the principal says to me over dessert. Her husband felt the same way when she got hired. Like he didn't exist, I ask, and she nods. I tell her about a boy at my preschool who always got left out. I thought it was sad, so I appointed him to be the door to our pretend grocery store. We would press him on the nose when we needed to go in and buy something. Opening, closing, the boy would mumble all recess long, and I tell the principal that that's exactly how I feel here. She thinks that it's completely natural to feel overlooked, because the students focus so intensely on their teachers. It's a phase all the trailing spouses go through, she says, and she hands me a cookie with a little bit of mold on it. Before what, I say. Before you learn to live with the situation, the principal says.

WHEN MY BOYFRIEND ties up a trash bag and carries it out to the trash can, he invariably thinks that I've filled it too high. It was a debate that we had to abandon after several years as a couple because we both simply stood our ground. I always think there's room for a little more trash, and my boyfriend's threshold is crossed many, many inches before my own. It's all about pressing it down, I would say, but my boyfriend would just shake his head. One trash bag gave way to another, and there was nothing more to say. All that was left was a faint little sigh. And yet, it is an important sigh. When he has to tear a new bag off the roll and fill it one third of the way up with the top of my trash mountain in order to make enough space to tie up the original bag, it is necessary for him to sigh. It must be said on his behalf that it is a nearly inaudible sigh, a close cousin of the heavy exhalation, but for an initiate there is no mistaking it. He feels no need to throw a fit as long as he can sigh. I smile affectionately when I hear it. You might say that I embrace his sigh, and, with a sincerity that I know he is both grateful for and suspicious of, I apologize, and I promise that I won't fill it so high next time. Hm, says my boyfriend, visibly pacified. We want it in Velling, and we know full well that we have shaped one another like landscapes. So we empty the dishwasher and we fill it again, our plates stacked like skyscrapers around the sink. We write out shopping lists that remain on the kitchen table, forlorn, when we arrive at the grocery store and install our son in a shopping cart. We wash hardened oatmeal off our wooden table and we buy a plastic tablecloth with smiling cows on it. We step down into a toy baby carriage with the full expectation that our foot will meet the floor, but instead we find ourselves rolling away, and a moment later we are lying on the floor and staring at the ceiling. Two spiders make their way toward one another from opposite sides of a spiderweb, as if they have an agreement to meet in the middle. We listen to the radiator's hum, the windmill's whisper, the gasping song of the thermos. The train thunders by under the bridge, and a bird flies into the window. It gets up in the garden, disoriented, and tomorrow it will again mistake our living room for the sky. The chorus practices a nocturne as it slowly starts to rain, and in the kitchen garden the wind passes through the cabbages, which shudder like lovers just parted.

Lost Am I Still
Love Song

Melody: You Were Born on Earth (Du fødtes på jord)
Composer: Erik Haumann, 1987

1 We met in the snow
   blinded by youth and with no way to know
   a whirlwind of joy and curiosity
   we met inside language, our sanctuary
   and there we have been
   again and again.

2 Again and again
   and the notes turned into a drawn-out refrain
   a plot, a story, a pop melody
   bedtime songs broken by the sirens' screams
   a tired affair
   a balloon without air.

3 A balloon without air
   a long run-on sentence beyond all repair
   I'm haunted so frequently by thoughts of flight
   but laughter spreads over your face like light
   you stretch out your limbs
   as morning begins.

4 As morning begins
   then we make the coffee and we drink it in
   and when we're assailed by chaos from all sides
   then we share a cigarette and roll our eyes
   and we ground our ships
   where the tenderness is.

5 Where the tenderness is
   we march in an army of unselfishness
   a love that's been worn thin by desperation
   borne only by hope and by dedication
   a time all askew
   my sleepy you.

6 My sleepy you
   my drama is long and my reason abused
   and when I get scared and when I get angry
   then sink my ships and bestow peace upon me
   the coast is in sight
   soon it will be light.

7 Soon it will be light
   so take me for granted now that calm presides
   for lost am I still though I've lived for so long
   and with gratitude do I sing this love song
   because, as you know
   we met in the snow.

The Day and the Road

IT'S GOT SOMETHING to do with right of way, I say, and I cast a quick glance down at my driving manual. Malte has a cigarette hanging out of his mouth and he carefully styles his curls so they'll look like they've fallen randomly. What's up, he says, stamping out his cigarette butt, when Mona's midnight-blue BMW pulls into the parking lot. Smoking's dangerous, says Mona, and she steps out of the car and lights a cigarette. Malte laughs, and I reach out for a drag of Mona's Camel Blue. None for you, she says, you've got a child, and she slaps my hand away. Mona hands me a little plastic car that she bought for my son. He'll probably end up getting his license before you do, she says. Malte laughs excessively. Let's get going, Mona says, and she directs me toward the bridge over the railroad tracks. I'm terrified of meeting an oncoming tractor or one of Vestas's many roaring transport trucks. It's the narrowest spot in Velling, and the road slopes treacherously so you can't see other vehicles until fifteen feet before you meet them in the middle of the bridge, where two cars can only barely get past one another. I say it's ironic that I happen to live by the only dangerous place in Velling. Mona says it would help me a good deal to stop imagining catastrophes everywhere I look. Why am I upset right now, she asks ten minutes later when I signal and turn to the left. She was supposed to yield, Malte says. Correct, says Mona, let's try again. Mona jokes that these suburban streets are no child's play, you never know what's around the corner. But seriously, she says, use your head, little mama. Malte laughs in the back seat, and I turn the car toward Tændpibe, where we catch a glimpse of a deer calmly grazing among the trees. Mona says that you should never try to swerve around a wild animal, it's simply too dangerous. She tells us about how a deer jumped at her out of the blue one time. It was looking her calmly in the eye, and one second later it was lying on the hood of her car. Its horns were broken, Mona says, and you know a deer has four stomachs, right. I shake my head. Yes, Malte says. Mona tells us that she's seen every one of them from the inside. The wipers were smearing blood across the windshield when the emergency workers showed up, and when they shot it, Mona heard the deer's loud cry from her seat in the car. Insurance covered it all, she says, but no one needs the image of a disemboweled deer imprinted on their retinas. I know that from now on I'm going to see phantom deer everywhere, deer with small fawns that won't make it back home to the woods alive, and my own head thrust against the windshield. Without thinking, I begin to drive more and more slowly, and I conjure a dark fantasy of how my son will become motherless, just like the baby deer. Cigarette break, yells Mona, and then you two can switch. How old are you again, she asks, looking at Malte. His face turns red and he smiles. Twenty, I say. Are you deaf, she says, and Malte shakes his head. Is she your ventriloquist, Mona asks, pointing at me. No, Malte says. His youth flutters around him like a small, beautiful bird. He stares at Mona when she speaks, as though her words were visible to him, as though they reached him through the eyes, and not the ears. Malte takes the wheel and we drive back toward the højskole. Everything the sunlight touches is yours, I whisper to him. The road lies ahead of us like a wall-to-wall carpet with stripes down the middle. He bites his lip and glances nervously in the rearview mirror. Nice driving, says Mona, you're right where you need to be. Malte turns bright red, he looks like he's trying to color-coordinate with the setting sun.

Dear Letterbox,

I've been married for eleven years and I'm getting tired of it, because my husband always insists on being right. We get along well for long periods of time, but his know-it-all attitude can make our coexistence challenging. For example, we just got home from a road trip that really brought out this negative trait in him. Every time we experience something new or unexpected he begins to hold a lecture about it instead of just living it. He's a man who knows a lot, but he certainly doesn't know everything. Should I threaten to leave him, or just accept my fate? Apart from this unfortunate characteristic, he's always been a loving husband and a good father.

Weary regards,

The Nitpicker's Wife

Dear Nitpickerwife,

I've never met your husband, and all nitpickers are different, but I would venture to guess that you, like me, live with a *factist*. It is an age-old diagnosis, and the word can be translated as: someone who derives pleasure from or to be enthusiastic about the truth. My boyfriend becomes nauseous when I generalize or simplify in an innocent attempt to get an overview of something. He looks at me sorrowfully and says that existence is more complicated than that. I've talked to him about how annoying it is to be corrected all the time, but, as a family member of a factist, you must understand that they just can't help themselves. While some may see them as arrogant, that would be an injustice. For factists, it's not about being right, it's simply an extreme sensitivity to facts. Precision is a way of life for them. Clearly, a factist ought to marry another factist, or at least someone who values their knowledge about the world. A great collision will take place if they live alongside a *feeloid*, who in this case is me and perhaps also you. I nourish a love of emotions, and I believe that you can unproblematically refer to them as basic truths. My advice, dear Nitpickerwife, is to try and have a little fun with the situation. I've noticed that my boyfriend's feet start to fidget when I exaggerate or repeat an anecdote imprecisely. If no one corrects me, the shaking in his feet grows increasingly violent, makes its way up to his knees, and spreads onward to his thighs. Finally, his shoulders begin to quake, and his head heaves from side to side. At this point the tremors are enormous. No, yells my boyfriend at last, no, that's not how it happened. All at once, his muscles relax, his body becomes completely still, and he slumps in his chair as if he's just experienced a particularly exquisite orgasm. I like driving my boyfriend crazy when he annoys me with his facts. It is a survival tactic, and it is my right. I sing a song that he knows, but I exchange one little word for another, a word that very much resembles the correct one, but is just a little off. The itsy-bitsy spider crawled up the water pipe, I sing, as our son claps along. My boyfriend looks sadly out the window, and later on I notice that he's downloaded a collection of children's songs. It's hard to tell whether this is a silent act of correction or if he just needed to hear the word *spout* before he could sleep at night. Right as he's slipping into dreamland, I mumble, as if asleep, that the Robert Bolaño book I'm reading is really good. My boyfriend gets up, suddenly wide awake, and shuffles out to the toilet. Roberto, I hear him whisper to his own reflection in the mirror, RobertO.

Sincerely,

The Letterbox

THE CHILDREN IN Maj-Britt's daycare are stationed on a bench in her garden, eating apple slices. How do you do it, I ask. Do what, Maj-Britt says. Keep them all so happy, I say, pointing to the future of Velling. The five children are sitting quiet as mice, and with their light curls and blue eyes they look like the front cover of a brochure for the Hitler Youth. We go for walks and we eat a lot, says Maj-Britt. She hands me a laminated piece of paper and says that there are some new initiatives in the child-and-youth sector. It's printed with butterflies and flowers, and in the middle is a photograph of my son, sitting open-mouthed on a lawn, looking like he just fell down from heaven. I learn from the text that my son, as a child in the Ringkøbing-Skjern municipality, aka The Kingdom of Nature, has attained a wide familiarity with common insects as well as small and medium-sized beetles. You are now the parents of a certified child of nature, it says in capital letters. Nor's mother comes in to the garden surrounded by her flock of children. You've really got your hands full, I say. She tells me that they run a slaughterhouse, and that it simply became necessary to have something tugging in the other direction, so they didn't get buried in pork chops. What a windy day, she says, and she crouches down in front of her son. Wow, I say, your hair is so beautiful. Thanks, yours too, Nor's mother says. And to think that you always wear it up, I say, you've been cheating us with those French braids you always strut around with. Nor's mother says that it's just more practical because she rides horses in her free time. She has two mares stabled out near Spjald. I start talking about

Wendy Magazine, which I read throughout my child-hood, and I try to remember some horse breeds. Nor's mother's horses are Arabians. Such reliable horses, I say. Exactly, Nor's mother says, and she asks if I've ever owned a horse. I say that I was mostly interested in Wendy as a person, and the horses were just a part of the package. I know it sounds crazy because it was just a cartoon, I say, but I thought Wendy was hot. I guess I got a little aroused, I say, not by the horses, I mean. I laugh aloud and say that bestiality has always been over the line for me. Nor's mother feels the same way, and she says she's disgusted by all the pimping of live-stock that goes on, which some farmers rely on as an extra income source when the harvest is bad. But do you think the animals actually feel anything, I ask. My certified child of nature pulls on my arm and points to the garden gate.

I KNOCK ON the door of Sebastian's practice room and go in. He has recorded the sounds of two slices of bread as they pop out of a toaster, and he's about to mix it with a recording of garbage bags falling through a trash chute. Sebastian plays the different sounds at high speeds one right after the other, and he explains that it's a commentary on food waste and consumer society in general. How is the trailing spouse doing, he asks. I think I may have lost the trail, I say, and I tell him about Saturday. In a total exception to the norm, our son fell asleep. We sat in the garden wrapped in blankets and drank sparkling wine, I say, and we had what one might call a moment. We shared a cigarette, the stars twinkled in the twilight, we said all the right lines. In other words, it was hyggelig. Suddenly, from offstage, a student came racing toward us like a zealous jogger, or a neurotic makeup artist who'd just noticed someone's eyeliner was crooked. But it wasn't, I say, it was Emma. And she was weeping. Why are they always weeping, Sebastian asks, and I shrug. I need to talk to you, Emma had said, pointing to my boyfriend. The students are under the impression that they own the teachers, an understanding that most of the teachers neglect to problematize. Within each of their subject areas, the teachers are idols, shining stars in a little højskole heaven. You're on our patio, and this is a private residence, I said. Emma stopped under the clothesline and stared at me, enraged. It's not such a good time right now, my boyfriend said. Emma said that it was important. I got up and found the phone number for the teacher who was on duty, but Emma said she didn't feel totally safe confiding in her. Tears ran down her cheeks, and my boyfriend stood up. What's up, he said. Can we take a walk, Emma whispered, and he followed behind her. Without the trailing spouse, I take it, Sebastian says. I nod. It turned out that Emma had broken up with Frej last week and she was consumed by guilt. In the meantime she had fallen in love with Mohammed, who was in a relationship with Petra, Emma's roommate. It's exasperating, I say. It certainly is, says Sebastian, who, like me, doesn't see it as a sign of defeat that our conversations mostly consist of us confirming perspectives that we fully agree upon. If only we were attracted to one another, then we would be compelled to have an affair as a matter of principle. But we're just two trailing spouses, Sebastian says, who would we trail then.

Dear Letterbox,

I am eight months pregnant and my finances aren't in the best shape. My husband and I have a good relationship and we're both in agreement that we need to have a spartan lifestyle until we get permanent jobs. We can get by as it is, but we've heard from a number of people that it would be smart for us to invest in a washing machine. We live on the second floor of an apartment building that has a perfectly fine laundry room. All the same, a lot of people think it's crazy to bring a child into the world without the ability to do the laundry within the four walls of one's own home. A few of my friends have gone so far as to say that you can't have a small child without a washing machine. Can you?

Sincerely,

The Pregnant One

Dear Pregnant One,

Congratulations on your coming child, and welcome to the chorus of whispers that pursues all new parents. Notice how people lower their voices when they talk about infants, as if you were sharing an intimate secret, a confidence for the chosen few. I heard this whisper for the first time when my son was four weeks old and I was breastfeeding eighteen hours a day. It feels like my breasts are about to fall off, I said, maybe I should give them a little rest. Nipple shield, the voices whispered, as if they had uttered something profane to my ragged breasts. It wasn't good, but it was better than the bottle, because the bottle was the Devil, and breastfeeding was God. These ominous vocal stylings returned when, months later, the conversation turn to porridge. Millet before oats, they whispered, or you'll ruin their stomachs. Yesterday my neighbor came for a visit and his daughter's cries were loud enough to split the living room in two. She's teething, he whispered, as if you would disturb the little tooth within her gums if you spoke too loudly. Crispbread, I chanted in the hushed voice that I've learned, it massages the gums. I've heard baby teeth take the blame for just about everything: screaming, crying, sleeplessness, fever, diaper rash, insane behavior. Personally, I don't think it hurts them when their teeth come in. I think it scratches a little, that it feels like a surprise in the mouth, but babies experience everything for the first time, and I doubt that teeth are any worse than so many other things. In any case, we need to get one thing straight. No one except a baby knows what it's like to be a baby. We can guess, we can research, but the only ones who know can't tell us. A friend waltzed into my house one day with a screaming-pink baby walker that he had found at a flea market. We set it up, put it in the middle of the living room, and christened it the emperor's chariot. My son loved it, and he would make joyful noises as he drove into our bookshelves at high speeds. It's bad for his back, the whispers said, he'll crush his hips if he uses that walker. I'm not sure what they imagined was happening. That we put my son in the emperor's chariot at dawn, that we just buckled him in and left him alone to roll the floors all day long. No midday nap, no pureed vegetables, no trips to the playground. When one of my boyfriend's colleagues saw it, she said it looked like it was from the early nineties. She shut her eyes, reached back into her memory, and said that she thought this brand was actually recalled from the market back then. She took pictures of the emperor's chariot and posted it on Facebook with a long text. My son stared at the walker fearfully and didn't make a sound. I put him up on my lap and started to feed him a salad with raisins. Whoa, said my boyfriend's colleague, and she grabbed my son's plate. Vegetables can get lodged in their lungs, she whispered, until they are three years old. Carrots were strictly forbidden, but our bad internet connection rescued the emperor's chariot. The colleague said she would research it at home and send us a message about whether we could keep it or not. It was in this period of time that I began to invent experts. They appear like little helpers when I have no desire whatsoever to get into a debate. I refer to pediatricians who don't exist, and parenting tips which I claim have been passed down through generations. A baby blog written by a mother of five, articles about childhood development that I stumbled upon online. New psychological studies show, I whisper, or, All experience indicates. Dear Pregnant One, there are so many truths. Find the principles that match your needs. Yes, you can bring a child into the world without owning a washing machine, but you'll need to get yourself an emperor's chariot. It should be ugly and pink, and it should remind you that your child's baby teeth will one day come loose. Like evil tooth fairies, we parents wriggle them out between threads of bloody gums. Some things in life can only be learned through experience.

Warm regards,

The Letterbox

IT'S WILD-GAME night at Hotel Skjern. The hunting season has started, and Krisser sensed an opportunity. The principal waves us off with our son in her arms when Cabbie-Connie comes in her taxi to pick us up. Welcome to the wilderness, Krisser says when I poke my head into the kitchen. I take a look at the various types of dead animals that are being rolled into and out of the kitchen. There are mallards, wood pigeons, deer, hares, bucks, and geese. Krisser asks the chef where all the side dishes are. Does my hotel look like a meatpacking plant, Krisser asks, does this seem vulgar to you. A little, I say, but the chef shakes his head. We have a salad on the menu, he says, but remember that we're in Skjern. The kitchen assistant, who is about to sprinkle walnuts over a platter of leafy greens and pomegranate seeds, is a part-time dietician. Arugula, Krisser laments, why. The assistant says iceberg lettuce is a victim of its own success, and she thinks that people just want to spice things up. I advise against condiment metaphors in a discussion concerning salads. Not the time, Krisser says, and she makes a horizontal motion over my mouth as if zipping my lips shut. She takes a handful of arugula leaves and considers them woefully. Is it still the nineties, Krisser asks, or do we find ourselves in the twenty-first century. The chef says that the culinary scene is a few years behind out west, just like the films they show at the movie theater. The chef's apprentice is standing off to the side, staring down at a frying pan in deep concentration. You're obsessed with your meat thermometer, Krisser says, and she pulls it out of a tenderloin before he has a chance to read it. She hides it behind her back and looks him in the eye. Do you have a girlfriend, Krisser asks. Yes, the apprentice says. The refrigerator hums, a pot of potatoes boils vigorously. Good, Krisser says, how long have you been together. Eleven months on Saturday, says the apprentice, and he takes his hat off as if he were standing guard at Amalienborg Palace, ready to salute the Queen. Congratulations, Krisser says, and she shakes his hand. How do you know whether your girlfriend is satisfied, she asks. I can just feel it, mumbles the apprentice. Precisely, Krisser says, and she throws the thermometer into the garbage. Gently, she places the tenderloin into the apprentice's hands. He caresses its seared surface in a state of confusion. Listen well, Krisser says, there's not a woman on earth who wants to be touched like that. The young man puts his hands on the tenderloin and massages it a little. Nice and easy, Krisser says, you don't want to go overboard. Rare, medium rare, or well done, Krisser asks. Medium rare, whispers the apprentice, and he carefully cuts a slice. Together they study the meat's surface. Perfect, Krisser says, and she puts his kitchen hat back on his head.

AS SOON AS Pia and Maria have brought us to our table, we start talking about our son. We find photos on our phone, imitate his facial expressions and grimaces. We've got to control ourselves, we say to one another, and we sing the praises of the mushroom sauce in an effort to change the topic. Gradually, we begin to talk about books, but it's a little unnatural, like we're trying to relearn a language we haven't spoken since childhood. To make matters worse, neither of us has read anything in an unthinkably long time. Something reminds my boyfriend of a little video he took on his phone of our son when he first laid eyes on a cow. We watch the clip a few times, and we show it to Pia, who calls Maria over. Here comes the good part, says my boyfriend. Our son's face metamorphoses from deep wonder into high-pitched jubilation when the cow lifts its tail and says moo. The woman at the neighboring table leans over and asks if he's our first. After a few minutes, she tries to go back to her rabbit ragu, but it's too late. I'm in the midst of an analysis of our one-year-old son's personality when I notice that she's staring vacantly at a point just above my nose. We rush to pay our check, and Cabbie-Connie drives us directly to Mylle's Café. My boyfriend gets us beers and I take over the jukebox, which makes me the enemies I've accustomed myself to making during my staggering journeys through the life of the night. I play Home to Aarhus and Moonlight Shadow, and then comes Childhood Street and A Thousand Pieces. Seriously, a group of high school students yell at me. You're a bunch of newborns, I say, you have no idea what music is. They scowl and make faces. Listen and learn, I say to the youth of the fjord. Later, we sit at their table and play a drinking game where my boyfriend and I have to take a shot every time one of us mentions our son. It's a bad habit and you all need to break it as soon as possible, says a girl the others call Chicken. Chug, chug, chug, the students yell. We turn into a time machine carrying our captive passengers back to the early two thousands. We wrote our assignments out by hand, my boyfriend says, and we looked up words in a dictionary made of sheets of paper. I take out a Prince 100 and pass the pack around the table. You could smoke everywhere, I say, and when we wanted to light a cigarette, we sat down and rubbed two pieces of wood together. When we buy a round for the table, Chicken says that she thinks we seem really young. If I didn't know better, I'd have thought you were twenty-eight, she says, smiling at me as if she'd just extended my life by four years. The night wears on to a soundtrack of Smurf hits and Britney Spears. Hit me, baby, one more time, we sing as we sway homeward along the darkened fields. We creep noisily through the entryway and open the door to our living room. On the sofa we see a sleeping principal and a sleeping baby. That's insane, my boyfriend says. Completely and totally insane, I say.

Dear Letterbox,

I must say that I find your tone to be very arrogant and, what's more, inappropriate. You make pronouncements on subjects you clearly know nothing about, and you mock people who are trying get to the bottom of things. As a pediatric nurse, I do a lot of work with small children. The reason that we monitor them is to make sure that they are doing well, and I feel compelled to correct your views on the "baby walker," etc. It is absolutely essential for the well-being of a little child that they do not walk before their nervous system is prepared for it. Furthermore, the "baby walker" presents a high risk of spinal injury because the child's lower vertebrae have not yet fully formed. The greatest sin of the "baby walker," however, is its irreversible consequence for vital neurological developments and for the roll-crawl continuum generally. It's worth noting that the National Board of Health itself advises against "baby walkers." You shouldn't play the expert on the topic of teething either, because all baby teeth are different. It has been proven many times that emerging teeth can lead to local infection, and that bacteria from the oral cavity can penetrate the gums at the site of tooth eruption, leading to symptoms such as sleeplessness, diarrhea, and diaper rash. Dear Letterbox, I willingly admit that "baby walkers" are a big hit with small children, and that it's possible to find pediatric health professionals hidden in the woodwork who will vouch for their positive influence on the development of motor skills. But take heed, because most people in the field would set it alongside the "baby jumper," which likewise stands accused of inhibiting normal development. Most nurses agree that the "baby walker" is harmful to the nervous system, and it also gives children a distorted sense of reality.

Sincerely,

Kirsten

Dear Kirsten,

Thank you for contacting me. Your opinions are hereby taken into account and passed on. I work every day on my arrogance, which, I agree, is not beneficial to my personality. I've noted your points of view, but I don't care for your tone.

Warm regards,

The "Letterbox"

GAS, GAS, GAS, Mona yells, you need to get up to eighty. My foot shakes on the pedal while Vellingvej glides by, flickering strangely. The fjord and the sky melt together, and my whole body is covered in sweat. I see an oncoming car and I immediately drive onto the shoulder. Stay in your lane, there's room for everyone, Mona hisses, and stay on the gas. Mona has cut down drastically on her smoking and now she's supplementing her nicotine intake with e-cigarettes. Put the clutch down, and shift up to fifth, Mona says, listen to the motor. She asks me if I can't hear that it sounds wrong. I shake my head, and she sighs. Signal to the right, clutch, and shift into second, Mona says, and she puts a hard candy into her mouth. With a pounding heart, I turn onto the pedestrian street. Take it slow, little mama, says Mona, the speed limit's only twenty in this zone, we need to get your pulse down. The sun shines on the citizens of Ringkøbing, who mill about happy and carefree. I am deathly afraid of all of these people, their baby strollers, roller skates, scooters, canes, and walkers. You're driving eight kilometers per hour, Mona says. Out the window I spot Anders Agger sitting with a young man at Italia, and I jerk up the emergency brake. Mona is thrust forward in her seat, and she screams at me. It's my blood sugar, I say, it's way too low. We sit down at the restaurant and order two Hawaiian pizzas. Even heroes have to eat, Mona says, and she takes a gulp of her soda. I yawn and try to see which pizza Anders Agger is eating. You look like a hanged cat, Mona says, is he still not sleeping. I shake my head. It appears to be a number ninety-one with tiger prawns, and I speculate as to what that might reveal about Anders Agger as a person. Mona says that he's really down to earth. I taught his daughter to drive myself, Mona says, and she didn't try anything. Try what, I ask. Shenanigans, Mona says. As I get up to go to the toilet, I make eye contact with Anders Agger, and a slight expression of shock passes across his face. Looks like it's pizza time, I say loudly, small world. Not all that small, says Anders Agger, and I think to myself that he looks very tired.

YOU'RE IN LOVE with Krisser, my mother says through the telephone, with her trenchant talent for drawing conclusions that are at once fully correct and completely wrong. I'm sitting in the hotel office and waiting for Krisser to find her bag, check her emails, and listen to her messages. Okay, are you ready, Krisser asks, as if she were the one waiting for me. We go down to the wine cellar, where she got her father-in-law to set up two armchairs. It's been a rough day, because Krisser has gotten a lot of helpful suggestions. Because most people have stayed in a hotel at some point in their lives they are convinced that they are experts. One guy from Skjern stopped her on the street to tell her that she was going over the top with her cuisine. People just want to eat pot pies, he said, they're back in style. Krisser had just finished *Ulysses* and she was considering celebrating Bloomsday by serving fried kidneys and hanging the Irish flag. She ran it by the hotel restaurant's chef, who looked back at her and said that that's not the sort of thing Mr. and Mrs. Skjern are after. I could also just have a buffet, Krisser yells, with thick brown sauce in a big bucket, boiled potatoes, and meat from mistreated animals, all you can eat for fifty-nine kroner. As if it weren't already trying enough to be a hotel director, her appearances make matters more difficult. My dimples are my curse, Krisser says, I look like a girl scout. And these don't do me any good either, she says, and she pulls on one of her dark-brown curls. At least it's not this nothing color, I say, tugging on my dirty-blonde braid. The missionary position of hair colors, Krisser says. There was a salesman who came by the hotel the other day and introduced himself at the reception desk. May I speak to the director of the hotel, he asked. You are, Krisser said. The man had a good laugh and repeated the question. She repeated the answer, and this cycle repeated itself several times. She opens a bottle of wine that they've just gotten in from a new supplier in Verona. Krisser wants to bring some culture to Skjern, and she thinks Sebastian and I should come and play our højskole songs. Future events take shape in Krisser's thoughts and bend themselves willingly to her desires, and I feel like a lump of dough in her hands.

Krisser's Song
Drinking Song

Melody: Good Night, You'd Better Go Home
(Go' nu nat og gå nu lige hjem)
Composer: Povl Dissing, 1981

A-part:

1 Hand in hand on the proud ship Drunkenness
forgotten are all worries and all stress
and for just a little while
cigarettes are back in style
and our reason is lost in the mist.

2 If you want to learn something about hotels
you'll find no answers hidden within yourself
I am trapped in a net
of taxes and budgets
it's not so simple, truth to tell.

3 We cheers and take a drink and then you say
that I am hyggelig, which makes my day
and I know that your hotel
will in time surpass itself
no dimples or curls can get in the way.

B-part:

4 We have breastfed, we have cried, we have sweat
we've been at one another's side no matter what
but the real challenge is
to run a hotel like this
on a tasteless and vulgar planet.

5 Your debt is large, your dreams are larger still
and your heart is as big as a hotel
with a will that's cast in iron
you've conquered the town of Skjern
before the ringing of the morning bell.

THE SAND DUNES rush by outside, and the windmills soar up like obstacles in my peripheral vision. Signal and turn, Mona says, it's not a merry-go-round. Right or left, I yell, clinging tightly to the steering wheel. Right, says Mona, we're on a roundabout. She looks at me with raised eyebrows and tells me to pull over. I barely manage to open the door before I throw up on the wet asphalt. I dry my mouth with the napkin Mona passes to me, and I say that it feels somehow shameful to get carsick from my own driving. White Sands is the town in Denmark with the most roundabouts per resident, Mona says. According to the traffic laws, you can take one turn around a roundabout, unless of course you've forgotten to turn off. Why, I ask. Otherwise people wouldn't do anything else, Mona says, and she looks up at the rearview mirror. She spent her teenage years drinking beers and driving around White Sands. We had God, fish, roundabouts, and not much else. I ask her if it drove her crazy. Sometimes it could get a little, she says. A little what, I ask. Ditchwater, Mona says. She starts the car again, and I drive us out onto Troldbjergvej. Keep your speed up, yells Mona. Finish your sentences, I say, you're impossible to have a conversation with. I ask how I'll ever get to know anyone here when the conversations all stop before they even get started. Mona rolls the window down and lights a cigarette. Tell me something about yourself, I say. She says that her boyfriend is a pediatric dentist in Rindum who is very preoccupied with oral hygiene. Morning and night he runs specially made plastic sticks around and around in his mouth, and afterwards he flosses for two minutes top and bottom. Every crumb of bread has got to go, she says, every grain of rice, every little string of meat, and every raspberry seed. And then it's time for Zendium. I hate Zendium, I say, no foam, no small hard explosions on your palate, just a thin white liquid filling your mouth. Exactly, says Mona, who is also a Colgate girl. What is he like otherwise, I ask. A straight shooter, Mona says, he won't give you any. Any what, I say. Bullshit, Mona says.

Dear Letterbox,

I am a woman in my mid-forties, and I have a big dilemma. I want with all my heart to meet my one and only, and I have been search-ing for him in vain for many years. It always feels promising at the beginning, but I've been the victim of cheating and lying so many times. How can I tell who these men really are? How can I sort the good from the bad on the first date so I don't keep getting hurt?

Sincerely,

The Victim

Dear Naïf,

Don't ask yourself who you want to marry, ask who you want to divorce. I'm talking about the whole package: broken dreams, couples therapy, moving boxes, family court, and, best-case scenario, a quick click on the citizen services website. Would he say, of course, just take the sofa, you've always loved it, or would he start sawing it in two in a rage, would he line the children up in two even rows and insist on having the first pick. And how would he describe you in his anecdotes. Would he let your shared memories rest in peace, or would you become the ex-wife he laughs about with his new girlfriend as they lie in the double bed eating scrambled eggs and bacon, encircled by the wide-eyed children you now share in joint custody. You can't judge people by how they treat you when you are out on a date, because you're showing one another the best versions of yourselves. The first sign you can be on the lookout for is very simple. How does your date treat other people, does he make jokes at the waiter's expense, is he arrogant, does he use a different voice when he places his order. Does he avoid eye contact and talk at the waiter like a microphone, a tube that runs back to the kitchen and automatically generates well-prepared dishes. Does he speak to the taxi driver like a GPS with voice-recognition software, where all you have to do is say the address that will guide you home. Or does he give a short but friendly smile when he tells the driver where he lives. I'm not talking about leaving massive tips or having long, intimate conversations. Common courtesy is sufficient, fifty kroner on the table when you leave the restaurant. Dear Naïf, consider your date's behavior toward people in the service industry, because they hold the key to his true nature. It is with them that everything begins and ends. Taxi drivers and waiters. Forget the wedding, remember the divorce.

Kind regards,

The Letterbox

MY BOYFRIEND AND I are practically hallucinating from sleeplessness. When someone asks us how we're doing, a wild look fills our eyes and we start to recite a precise account of the previous night. We can turn every conversation back to sleep. All sleep patterns are different, the pediatric nurse tells us when we call her. I've lost the ability to spell, and suddenly I can't remember what the most ordinary words look like. When my son finally sleeps, I dream that he has woken up, and I dash to his crib, my heart pounding. I move through the world like a sleepwalker, the slightest noise sends me into a panic, and I live in fear that the world will come crumbling down on top of me. I consult the principal, who has two grown daughters. We take a walk down Røde Bro, surrounded by fields, the wind whipping through our hair. She says it was a different era back when she had kids. People smoked during pregnancy, there were no baby alarms, and children were just a natural part of one's life. In the evenings she would push two chairs together and the girls would fall asleep in the assembly hall to the sound of music and dancing. But that was thirty years ago, I say, could it be that you've forgotten a few of the details. The principal says that she doesn't think so, that she's always had an excellent memory. I ask whether she thinks that the laissez-faire parenting of that era gave rise to the neurotic parents she is a witness to today. The principal says that every generation does things their own way, and that's the way it should be. Imagine if we lived in the Stone Age, I say, as I rock the baby carriage up and down. I try to hit the uneven ground on the side of the road so it will bounce the carriage as much as possible. My son shuts his eyes for a moment, but he opens them as soon as I stop the rocking. The principal says that, in that case, my boyfriend and I would've likely been abandoned by our tribe and left alone with a screaming baby, which would attract wild animals. A few weeks ago, she invited us to a dinner she was hosting for some Icelandic painters who were visiting the school. Her husband had prepared a five-course meal and all the candles were lit. I had tried to fit a mascara brush between my drooping eyelids, and my husband took a shower. Our son sat in my arms at the table and smiled, clearly captivated by a decorative salad. Isn't he sweet, one of the guests said. No, my boyfriend and I said in unison. We were trying to be funny, but I think we were both surprised at how bitter we sounded. All the same, we couldn't stop. We joked about putting him up for adoption or finding him a loving foster family here in Velling, and we laughed with a loud, shrill laughter that I could hear but I couldn't control. All evening long we brought every subject back to sleep, which was an impressive feat as the guests were interested in nearly every aspect of Danish society. After a long deliberation over whether to lay the blame on our thin curtains or potential gastrointestinal issues, and speculating as to whether the dust from the gravel road may be playing a role, we realized that everyone else had fallen silent. If we could just get him to use a pacifier, my boyfriend mumbled. A mute weariness had settled over the faces of the six guests. The principal poured wine into the tall glasses and smiled apologetically to her guests. I looked into my boyfriend's eyes and at that moment we were the only two people on earth, but it wasn't like when we first met. It was like two people who simultaneously grasp the fact that they are dangerously ill, that they need to be locked away before they can infect others. We put our son into his baby carriage out in the entryway and packed his diaper bag. We could hear the conversation gradually begin to pick up again in the dining room, and it was when someone laughed loudly that I realized the people around us had long stopped laughing altogether. The lullabies took on an aggressive intonation that night, tensions rose, and we passed our son back and forth between us like a trophy no one wanted to claim. Our googling grew desperate, developing from: How do you get a baby to sleep, to, long after midnight: How early can you identify a personality disorder. We spoke openly of our revenge fantasies. How, in sixteen years, we would wake our son with giant gongs whenever he had a hangover. We would go around the house playing the trumpet after he'd stayed up all night gaming and eating cheese puffs. In an instant of undiluted evil, we wished that he would one day have a healthy, happy baby who never slept a wink. When he one day came to understand what he had done, and called us to apologize, we would take a deep breath and say: Ah, those nights, but that was so many years ago. We would display our benevolence, affirm that we bore no grudge, but we would also make it clear that we expect an exceedingly comfortable old age. Frequent visits to the nursing home and souvenirs from all of his trips. A soft bed when the end is near, gentle songs, and unconditional love until we ourselves close our eyes.

I'M STARING OUT of the front window of our car and listening to a radio program about the history of jazz. A stuffed rabbit sits in the car seat behind me, and I can feel its glass eyes on my neck like an impatient prickle. I look into a house, at what must be the kitchen. A silhouette stands up and moves around, reaches its arms up to some shelves and pours something into some thing else, neither of which I can make out. We make eye contact through the two window panes. I get out and wave my arms, pointing to the car and raising my hands to the sky. Anders Agger comes out of the house. It just stopped, I say in a strange-sounding voice. Okay, he says, and he gets into the car. Anders Agger turns the key and points to the dashboard. It might have something to do with the fact that the battery is dead, he says, pointing at a little icon. Well how about that, I say, maybe I forgot to turn off the light when I stopped to answer my phone. I tell him that I'm really close to getting my driver's license and that I cruise around the back roads for practice. He nods slowly and gets himself out of the car. It's not like I'm some kind of sick stalker, I say. What are you then, Anders Agger asks. The gravel crunches beneath my feet, and I shrug my shoulders. Do you want to tell me an idea for a documentary, Anders Agger asks. He is often sought out by people eager to shed light on a particular topic. I shake my head and say that I'm just a transplant, and I'm having a hard time talking to the Velling locals. Anders Agger concedes that the flow of conversation may be a bit different, and he says that, in contrast to everyone else, he has the opportunity to edit the pauses out of his programs. That's a cheap trick, I say, and I criticize him for giving a distorted picture of reality. To be honest, I think the people of West Jutland have a negligent relationship with communication, I say. A different one than you in any case, says Anders Agger. Even the names of the towns are terse, I say, Tim, Hee, Noe, Bur, Lem, Spjald, Tarm. Vemb, Asp, Tvis, Skjern, says Anders Agger, and he drums his fingers against the roof of the car. In Velling most people work with the wind, the earth, or animals, he says. Nature doesn't talk back, and that can be contagious when you live here. You can't translate the fjord, Anders Agger says, it just sits there. You can compare it with love, how when people try to define it, they go wild in a jungle of metaphors. It's impossible to articulate the kind of power that compels teenagers to lay down on train tracks and intelligent people to speak in baby talk. It seems like you navigate between people so easily, I say, scratching at a spot of bird poop on the windshield, I just wanted to ask if you could give me some tips. Anders Agger smiles at me and, befittingly, he does not protest. I think I just like them, he says, people. Does that mean you like me too, I ask. I think so, says Anders Agger, but you have to stop following me around, it'll get too weird in the long run. Cheers, I say. Anders Agger says he'll have to make us some coffee before he can say it back.

Dear Letterbox,

I'm a twenty-six-year-old woman with a big problem. My best friend has repeatedly told me that I've let her down. Her complaining is hurting our relationship, and I have a hard time relaxing when I'm around her. I've been afraid to bring it up because she's going through a rough period. Three weeks ago I forgot her birthday, and now she's asked me if we can take a walk around the lake on Sunday, but I just don't want to listen to her criticisms. Am I a bad friend? How can I break this vicious cycle?

Sincerely,

The Confused One

Dear Confused One,

Be careful with lakes. There's something about the water, something about the circles, that lends them to conversations people would rather have outside of the home. Lakes promise discretion and intimacy, lakes promise to solve your problems. Personally, I have a hard time with lakes, because they attract people like your friend. This isn't supposed to be about me, but I know what you're going through. I used to have a friend called Kasper. He was very sensitive and he analyzed every little thing. When he called to ask if you could meet him at the lake, you knew exactly what you were in for. His voice would have a certain timbre, tones of mild complaint on a foundation of something resolute. I could always tell that the conversation had already been acted out in his head. The pauses were deliberate, his lines carefully rehearsed in advance. I knew there was probably something I had said in an insensitive way, either that or a personal crisis, the extent of which I had not grasped. I'm not saying I am innocent. Like most late-modern people, I'm only a good friend when I'm bored or in need of others. But it must be said that Kasper was full of emotions. They needed to be taken out for a walk, like a litter of unruly puppies. He wore them on his sleeve, they darted around him as he walked, and they ravaged everything in his path. They rampaged like wild teenagers, had unprotected sex and propagated themselves, formed a street gang which ambushed innocents and left their victims helpless. Every once in a while I tried to mollify them. I'm sorry,

I said. I'm sorry I wasn't there for you when your great-uncle died, I didn't realize that you were so close. I'm sorry I laughed at the book you gave me for my birthday. I know I'm a snobby elitist, it was insensitive of me, I'm sorry. Dear Confused One, stay in your own lane, and stay away from the lake. Nature is not neutral, it has a will, and the lakes of Denmark are a blue Monday's tears, filled with mascara and dissolved powder. They masquerade as clean and pure, untouched by the world, but we all know that most of them are artificial. Nature preens itself here as the clock counts down, the earth coughs one last time before lying down to die. But of course you can become sentimental at the thought of life's fleeting nature. You gently pull into the slow lane. You drink red wine, you listen to Anne Linnet, and it suddenly occurs to you that you have a pretty good voice, that she may be in need of a backup singer. *If you once called me a friend, chances are I'm still here for you,* you sing around the campfire on a summer night. Someone plays guitar, and it all brings tears to your eyes, because you feel full of forgiveness. The next day you call Kasper, and he sounds happy, but then he sets off an inquiry into how he's really doing, whether he's truly listening to himself. Then we drink another round with all our friends. We watch people meeting and parting, creating dramas and resolving them again. We take a deep breath. The swans are swimming, the sun is shining, and we know that there is lake water for everyone, and words as far as the eye can see.

Warm regards,

The Letterbox

MAJ-BRITT IS LOOKING at me expectantly, she wants to plan her Easter break. I'm sitting at the bench in her kitchen, making eye contact with a little snowman that's wearing Bent's earmuffs. Its smiling mouth is made out of an apple slice, and it reaches toward me with its twig fingers. It's the middle of December, I say, no one knows where they'll be in four months. But Maj-Britt knows, she knows that Tarm is where she wants to be in week sixteen. I'm so tired of numbering the weeks, I say, the calendar system works flawlessly, use it. Maj-Britt says that they need to let the substitute daycare teacher know, and that it takes more planning than you might realize. There are a lot of balls in the air, she says, you've got to keep your wits about you. I say that I refuse to be a part of a society that's obsessed with scheduling every detail, and Bent says he doesn't think I need to worry about that, with the job I have. He's in the process of butchering a pig on the kitchen table, an early Christmas gift from Nor's parents. How's business, asks Bent, who is a faithful reader of my advice column, even though he can't quite believe that I consider it to be a real job. When he talks about me getting paid for it, he always laughs a little, as if I've really bamboozled the newspaper. He says that my responses are a bit on the long side, but the one with the taxi driver and the waiter, that was a good one. Shouldn't you be wearing a ring soon, says Bent as he cuts open the pig's ribcage. You've come this far, you might as well finish the job, he says, pointing into the playroom. I say that I earn my living by giving good advice, and I have no need for more when I'm finally off. Bent tells me that

146

there are considerable tax advantages when it comes to marriage. I say that I'm a socialist and I pay my taxes gladly. You've just got to light a fire under him, Bent says. I roll my eyes over to the dead pig's face and I call for my son. Just focus on your pig, Bent, says Maj-Britt.

THE TEACHER WHO was on duty has gotten sick, and I've promised to provide transportation for Emma, who has a doctor's appointment in Ringkøbing. We're waiting for a taxi at the main entrance, and she says it's crazy how long it's taking me to get my license. The students are placing bets on when I'll pass the test, and they're putting the money in a pool. Soon we'll have enough for a trip to Cuba, Emma says, and she takes her health card out of her wallet. What is it that you need to see the doctor about, I ask. The ceramics teacher had told me that Emma had gotten chlamydia, and not to ask her about it. It's a kind of virus, Emma says with an angry look. Oh, where is it, I say, it doesn't sound good, but you don't seem all that sick. She lights a cigarette and says that you can tell I've quit smoking. Your fingernails look like ragged corncobs, Emma says, and you seem totally unstable. Outdoor education and green entrepreneurship troop across the parking lot with flushed cheeks. They've been out gathering edible herbs for a climate-friendly soup they're going to make with culinary arts. It will be sold in town, where, along with a group of local activists, they've arranged a peace protest. It's also a protest against Christmas, Emma says. She finds it distinctly creepy that we uncritically pass on this whole story of a white, middle-aged man who comes flying down from the sky and gives presents to privileged children. I say some people might contend that Christmas is about the birth of Jesus, but for Emma he's just another representative of the patriarchy. The students are going to march with candles and sing songs on the square. I say that I'm sure it will get the dictators and thugs of the world to stop in their tracks and reconsider their actions: maybe that genocide wasn't such a good idea, maybe violence isn't the answer. Emma says that my boyfriend actually thinks it's a really important statement. He is employed to encourage you, I say, don't ever forget it. Are you still writing for that women's magazine, she asks as she stamps out her cigarette. Newspaper, I say, it's an advice column, and it requires the wisdom of experience to write it. Cabbie-Connie turns into the parking lot and honks three times in quick succession. The time of oracles has passed, Emma says, and she gets into the back seat.

Dear Letterbox,

I'm a young man in my teens and I've just gotten into my first real relationship. We're really happy together, but my girlfriend cries a lot. I try to comfort her, and sometimes it helps, but not always. She can cry about anything, and not only during a fight or a disagreement. I've cried two times in front of my girlfriend, but before that I had never let anyone see me in tears. Is it true that it's healthy to cry, and do you think she'll get over it?

Best wishes from a raft inside the tear ducts

Dear Rafter,

Taking your ages into consideration, I don't think you need to worry. My first love had big, almond-shaped eyes. Not only were they deep as a forest lake, but they were full of small schools of fish that shone like swift, silver daggers, swaying aquatic plants, and northern pike stalking their prey. The rains of summer dripped down, and, as our drama grew in those years, a new and wonderful world of catastrophes sprang forth. The tears rolled between us, turned into the puddles in which we splashed, Randers Fjord at sunrise. When we felt even a minimal distance between us, we wept, even though it probably meant nothing except that, despite our best efforts, we were two different people. I think I cried more during the three years that Nanna and I were together than I will for the rest of my life. We kept on crying for many years, when we would meet at a café or with mutual friends. How are you, she would say, and I would start crying. How about you, I would ask, and the tears would roll down her cheeks. She continued to speak directly to my sixteen-year-old heart, and it answered her without hesitation in the same language. Now that we have children we've stopped crying, and if we do get to talk, it's when Nanna is driving the stretch of road from her office out to Mårslet. I'm home now, she'll say, let's talk soon. Dear Rafter, we cry less with age, but it's not necessarily a good thing. One day you will miss your tears.

Warm regards,

The Letterbox

MY LESSON TODAY is called Heavy Traffic in Herning, and I'm going to learn to keep my head on straight in stressful situations. They call it the Las Vegas of Jutland, Mona says as we pass by the town's welcome sign. I yawn. I feel like fatigue is constantly jumping out at me in a new disguise, I say to Mona, it forces itself into every single state of mind. The combinations are endless: my boyfriend and I can be tired and angry, tired and confused, tired and stressed, or tired and happy, like after a long day of sledding when you were a child, rosy cheeks and hot chocolate right before you go to bed. Tired like marathon runners, sweaty and drained, but also proud. We are two politicians presenting our absolutely final offers, our cigars stubbed out, our cognac glasses half-full. Tired like two slow bodies which, at the same time, bend down to pick up a rain-soaked newspaper, like dentures that smile to one another from their separate glasses of water. Sleeplessness is making our features blur, turning us into strange clones of ourselves, and when we get so tired that we won't ever wake again, our final yawn will be as vast and quiet as death itself. Does that sound normal, I say. Yes, Mona says, her boyfriend has a son and two little girls from a previous marriage. At night they crawl into the double bed and roll back and forth until Mona nearly loses her mind. You ought to have a prize, I say, and I cast a glance in the rearview mirror, which blinds me with sunlight. I have three, Mona says. We practice left turns, and I shriek as if I were sitting in a breakneck roller coaster as Herning slowly takes me into its clutches. Gas, yells Mona, and cyclists swarm around me like pesky insects. The turn lanes are full of them, and pedestrians pop up out of the blue. Herning is a ball of yarn bouncing from wall to wall, ready for action. It's the Dubai of Denmark, but stuffed with bacon, buffets as wide as boulevards, trumpets blaring in the heavy traffic.

THE ICE CREAKS beneath my feet, and the wheels of the baby carriage roll across the frozen fjord. Krisser and I walk side by side, and our breaths turn into big clouds ahead of us. Krisser is freezing. She wants to go home to her sofa. She refers to it as if it were an equal member of the family, and when she calls me on her way home from work, it sounds like a beloved person she will be reunited with. The sofa is the opposite of a faulty alarm system that goes off in the middle of the night, the opposite of unreliable employees who drift by like extras on a movie screen. It is a little island where Krisser and her family lie as they look out at the greenhouse that fills half of the garden. Karsten was Krisser's teacher at culinary school and a part-time winegrower. During the orientation week he had organized a wine tasting with different types of pinot noir for the first-year students. The cultivation of the grape can be traced back further than our calendar systems, he said, but it's sensitive, it's easily affected, it takes a lot of care. Notice how thin the skin is, he said, and he pointed to his PowerPoint, which was zoomed in on a blue grape. You can walk me home, but don't try anything, Krisser said after she had tasted three varieties from California and eight from France. She locked the door to her bedroom and sent Karsten off to the sofa. It was from IKEA, oddly beige, and five feet long. The next morning Karsten had back pain and a severe hangover. I'm never doing that again, he said. Two days later there came a knock on the door. When Krisser opened it, Karsten was standing behind a beautiful and very large sofa, which they carried into her apartment together. In lieu of flowers, he said, as they sat next to one another and caught their breath. Aw shucks, Krisser said, and she gave his arm a little punch. It was dark red, so you wouldn't be able to see any future wine stains, and Krisser says that if there's one thing about Karsten that she really values, it's that he plans ahead. So I kept them both, she says, and she looks down at Vera's baby carriage. The children have fallen asleep, and together we walk back toward Velling. The town's welcome sign is reflected in her eyes, and there is a beautiful simplicity to her outlook, which allows for no doubt. I'll probably never figure out why, but it's as if the events in her life don't assume the bizarre proportions that constitute my existence. Today I want nothing more than to collapse into this peace by Krisser's side.

Song for a Snowless Winter
New Year's Song

Melody: The Wind Blows Fresh over Limfjord's Waters
(Blæsten går frisk over Limfjordens vande)
Composer: Povl Hamburger, 1937

1 January blows its restless will
over the icy sea and fjord
like a broken family, confused and shrill
the seagulls scream in sad discord
and every creature is trapped in the cold
alone with the darkness and winter's scolds.

2 January's lies will be forgotten
long board games you never won
songs that are sung in voices uneven
woven hearts that are shoddily done
a year is past, abandoned and confounded
a table deserted that once was surrounded.

3 January holds in its hand a glove
  it breathes deep as the sky benighted
  our breaths rise like smoke above
  though no cigarette was lighted
  we cough and we sneeze, we are in such pain
  the ghost of summer wanders in vain.

4 January waves farewell to the land
  icicles sparkle like lights on the eaves
  tho fjord freezes over, we walk hand in hand
  and day by day the night retreats
  the spring will come and the fjord will flow
  as flowers awake in the melted snow.

IS THIS SOME kind of parent-teacher conference, I say as I sit down at the usual table in The Main Office. The surfer from Søndervig has a guilty look on his face as he puts a chocolate milk in front of me. You've been asleep at the wheel, Mona says with a smile, her teeth shockingly white. You can't even drive forwards into a parking space anymore. I take a french fry from her plate, the surfer holds a little cup of remoulade out for me, and I dip it carefully. Your left turn has gone to the dogs, Mona says, and remember that it's also dangerous to drive too slowly. At our last lesson Mona had grown more and more frustrated. That's the fifth eighteen-wheeler that's passed us, she yelled at last. I yawn, and it's impossible for me to tell whether the bread on the surfer's plate has crumbled or my vision is blurry. The fact is, you're disrupting traffic, Mona says, society is grinding to a halt because your son doesn't sleep. But don't worry, we still support you, she says, and the surfer nods his head. Your case has become a matter of principle, Mona says, and she shuffles through some papers. Seventy-two extra lessons, she says, it adds up. The surfer says he once had a student who turned to hypnosis, and he's also heard that acu-puncture can help with the fear. He looks at me and raises his hand for a high five, but Mona swats him away. Not now, she says, taking her glasses off. I've got to throw in the towel, Mona says, it's too much for me to handle in the middle of quitting smoking. She ex-plains that even though she's gone all in on e-cigarettes, her stress threshold is low at the moment. It's Parking Peter's turn, Mona says, and she passes him the folder with my driving records. She gets up from the table and pats me on the shoulder. I'll see you around for beers and e-cigarettes, she says, and she disappears into Brejningvej's roundabout.

AS I ENTER the daycare, I see my son sitting in the playhouse in the backyard. Maj-Britt and Bent are standing side by side with their backs to me, looking out at him, and they seem like a picture, framed by the window. On the kitchen table are the remains of a cake and a big box of chocolates. Ella has had her last day, and now she's going to preschool. What wild weather, Bent says, taking his glasses off, so much for springtime. The snowdrops are vibrating outside, and the wind makes the world look tentative and random. It goes by so fast, says Maj-Britt, you look up at the sky to see if they need their rain jackets on, and when you look down again, they're gone. Twelve meters per second, Bent says, according to the Meteorological Institute. Maj-Britt nods. They've got to move on, she says, that's how it is. Her nurturing instincts are uprooted, they have to find new pathways, new little people to love. Ella, on the other hand, doesn't yet know the meaning of goodbye, and she lacks the imagination to conceive of anything but a world where Maj-Britt will also await her at preschool, or where Ella herself will, in a sort of parallel universe, attend both daycare and preschool. Maybe she will pester her mother into visiting Maj-Britt a few times, but before long she will become shy. She will think she's returning to a well-known place, but something within her will have changed. Her body will grow, and the little yellow coat hook and her cubbyhole will now belong to another, smaller child. She will hide her face in her mother's skirt, and try to make herself invisible. The visit will turn into a burden, it will feel wrong, and indeed, almost impossible. Maj-Britt will smile at Ella. She still knows her children, and they are two people who will always share something, even if the smaller one will forget most of it. And just as Maj-Britt will always have a place in the earliest memories of her daycare children, they will also leave something behind with her. Their special natures, speech impediments, various levels of stubbornness, their hysterical fits and sleepy smiles. During the first period of their human lives, Maj-Britt is a firmly rooted tree in the wind, a calm that the children will, without knowing it, take with them. When they have their last day at daycare, Maj-Britt will stand in the doorway and wave until she can't see them anymore, and that's how they will remember her, peaceful and unchanging, like the best childhood memories.

Dear Letterbox,

I am a man in my early thirties, and I'm often afraid. Fear can strike down on me like lightning from a clear blue sky, without any visible cause. I still haven't found the right woman and I'm worried that I'll die lonely and alone. My family supports me a lot, and I have plenty of good friends. I feel like everyone else has everything figured out. Why do you think it's so hard for me?

Sincerely,

The Virgin

Dear Virgin,

My driving instructor told me that my fear of death won't do any good if it ends up killing other people, and she passed me off to another instructor. He was born patient, she said, and he knows that you're scared shitless. A part of me would like to know exactly what Mona said to him, because even the way Parking Peter buckles his seatbelt strikes me as pedagogical. He addresses me like a hybrid between a small child and a psychologically unstable person, and he seems genuinely impressed whenever I shift gears. Very nice, he says if I put my signal on before I turn. I know his profile better than I know his face, because we're always staring out of the windshield, both committed to surviving the day's lesson. When he turns his head toward me, I'm always surprised that his face is symmetrical. That there are two eyes, and a smile that continues over on the other side. I'm still afraid of sudden roadworks and schoolchildren, but when I sit down next to Parking Peter, it's like something falls into place, my breathing changes and becomes regular. I'm well aware of the confusion I cause at intersections, and at the beginning I thought it must be incomprehensible for Parking Peter, who, practically speaking, lives in his car. One day between Højmark and Lem, he cleared his throat and told me that he and his brother once traveled to the USA. In Arizona they took a helicopter tour over the Grand Canyon, suddenly it began to thunder and lightning. Everything was going wrong, the pilot looked nervous and was trying to radio in an emergency message. Peter and his brother sat completely still and clung to their seats. When they finally landed, the pilot took his cap off and looked at them. He made the sign of the cross and shook both of their hands. This is just to say that I can also be scared, Parking Peter said. Dear Virgin, everyone has their fears, but you have to surround yourself with people who hold your neuroses in check. Try to find someone who can get you to believe that traffic is one big, benevolent creature that, fundamentally, just wants everyone to arrive on time.

Warm regards,

The Letterbox

THREE MINUTES, ANDERS Agger says, and he presses the button on his stopwatch, getting better. We've been sitting in silence on a bench in front of the fjord. He asks if I can see how you can get used to it. I shrug, and it's like my words have completely vanished. We're doing conversation tempo training and drinking coffee from a thermos. Anders Agger says that if you want to get close to rural people, the focus should be on unremarkable details. Scenario number one, he says. My dog has been hit by a car and you meet me by chance at the grocery store. I hesitate a little and then ask how he's doing. Fail, Anders Agger says, far too personal, and for god's sake stop looking into my eyes like you're trying to hypnotize me. Now it's your turn, I say, and Anders Agger clears his throat. Shame about the dog, he says, while looking off over my shoulder. If you absolutely must dig for more, then mention that it's always tough when a dog dies. Third person before second, Anders Agger says, the situational before the personal. He explains you grant the other party a freedom in that little distance. It's important and must be respected, because there aren't that many people in Velling. In big cities you try to distinguish yourself, to be noticed, but in small towns the goal is to blend in and become a part of the landscape. People cultivate their commonalities instead of their differences, subtly refer to their mutual interests, that's the purpose and logic of these conversations. I see, I say, and I take notes on my telephone. And then there's the modesty, he says, you've got to keep everything that has to do with the body behind a watertight seal. Birth, I ask, menstruation, exercise. Everything, Anders Agger says, unless it's about a serious illness. He asks if he can give me some good advice. Never talk about reproduction, Anders Agger says, and he looks at me gravely, sex is a no-go in the public sphere. I say that I wish I had met him earlier in my life. He clinks his thermos cup against mine. He sets his stopwatch without telling me how long. It's like playing cards, I say, but without the cards. You've just got to keep your cool, Anders Agger says, if you stay silent for long enough then eventually they'll start to talk.

HOW FAST CAN you drive in a roundabout, Parking Peter asks me, raising one eyebrow. Fifty max, I mumble. You were going eighty, he says, and he lifts his foot from the instructor's brake. I didn't see it, I say, it jumped out in front of the car. Some of the students are cautious and have to get used to being behind the wheel, others are reckless and have to learn to listen to traffic, but you, you're unpredictable, Parking Peter says. He sounds almost impressed. You have the traits of a beginner, a senile person, and a getaway-car driver. A car honks behind me, and Parking Peter leads me through a left turn before we park in front of a convenience store. Wait here, he says, and he comes back with two cinnamon buns. I feel an unexpected communion with him when I discover that we have the same technique. We bite rightward around the outermost ring, slowly approaching the glaze at the center. Do you think that says something about us as people, I ask. No, Parking Peter says. He turns his head and seems to study me. You're not a good driver, he says, but your driving is remarkable. Peter appears to me for the first time not just as a driving instructor, but as a person, a father, a neighbor, a friend. Do you think I'll ever get my license, I ask him right before the glaze. One day at a time, Parking Peter says, and he hands me a massive Toblerone chocolate bar he picked up in Germany. I accept it as if it were a paddle being reached out to me, a lifeboat in a churning sea.

Dear Letterbox,

I'm an eleven-year-old girl, and I think my classmates treat me badly. They never ask me if I want to play, and when they do I'm not sure if they're just making fun of me, because I'm terrible at sports. They leave me out and laugh at me during class. My father says that they're not real friends. I would rather have bad friends than no friends, but that's hard for people to understand who aren't kids themselves.

Best wishes,

The Lonely One

Dear Lonely One,

I wish it were otherwise, but unfortunately I have to agree with your father. Better to do without than to settle, as my mother is wont to say. Of course, this doesn't apply to all aspects of life. If your favorite muesli is sold out, then you buy the one with dried cranberries. If the kiosk is out of Prince 100s, you can make do with Camel Golds. Everyone is acquainted with the mild irritation of second best, but when it comes to friends, there can be no compromising. Sit down and read some books, that's what I did during my entire childhood. I always brought a book to birthday parties, I crawled under the table and ate cake while I read. I was actually enjoying myself, but suddenly I had to talk to a psychologist and draw pictures of my parents. I looked over at my mother, who winked at me, and I drew a happy sun above my stick figures. She just likes to read, my mother said, there's nothing else to it. The psychologist took his glasses off and nodded. Dear Lonely One, not everyone has a talent for childhood, and it's nothing to be ashamed of. If you don't possess an innate lightheartedness, then childhood can feel a little long, I'll be the first to admit it. The good news is that one is an adult for longer than one is a child, and adults have more avenues for escaping loneliness. You can try sex or alcohol, but usually it's easier to just communicate, because, in spite of it all, most people become more civilized with age.

Warm regards,

The Letterbox

THE PRINCIPAL HAS gotten some cones from the gymnasium and placed them around the parking lot with plenty of room between. You need to turn the wheel halfway to the right, Malte says, and he reminds me to check my side-view mirrors. He had a night driving lesson with Mona yesterday and he's still completely beside himself. They had practiced putting the high beams on as they drove around the curving country roads. Malte has taken the driving test three times, and it has gone well, but every time, he has driven through a red light just before the test was going to end. You're a man possessed, I say, and he nods. I was once very much in love, I say, and it was like I was haunted by brown eyes. They were everywhere, and I was especially afflicted in the mornings. The raisins in my oatmeal, a handful of hazelnuts, the coffee grounds I wiped out of the sink, everywhere I looked. Malte says that that's how it is for him with the midnight-blue BMW, he dreams about it at night. Malte starts the car and puts my hands on the wheel. I see my boyfriend walk by with our son in the side-view mirror just as I knock down a cone. I roll down the window and say that if you fall for someone, it's a question of timing and, ultimately, endurance. I see, Malte says. Are you preaching, my boyfriend asks. It's our duty to preach, I say, and our son stretches his arms out toward me. Malte wants to go to The Main Office, so my boyfriend buckles our son in and takes the wheel. I've moved up in the food chain, I say to Malte, it's me who catches the wildebeests so that you can have something to eat. But Malte is a vegetarian, and he orders a plain bun after we take our seats at a table next to the driving instructors. When we die, our bodies become the grass, my boyfriend says, and the antelope eat the grass. Small world, Mona says, and she slides over so that we can join her at their table. Not that small, I say, and Malte concentrates on our son's hot dog, cutting it into pieces and blowing on them.

MY SON IS still taking his afternoon nap, and I'm waiting for him to wake up while Maj-Britt plants spring bulbs in her flower pots. Pansies and Lenten roses, she says, and she shows me some pictures from a gardening magazine. Doesn't it make you jealous, I say, pointing at two flies having passionate sex on my knee. Nor's mother, who has just come through the gate, says they're not getting seasick in the waterbed at her house either. After discreetly asking around at her riding club, she slowly came to the conclusion that it was perfectly natural. The heavy sigh of life itself, I ask. Nor's mother shrugs her shoulders. Pigs, horses, children, and a long sex life had worn them thin and tired them out. Their intercourse felt like a product of goodwill and firm planning. Nor's mother tells us about one morning when the neighbors were looking after the children. Nor's mother's wife kissed her, but she couldn't stop thinking about the chicken she had just taken out of the freezer, and whether it would have time to thaw out by the time her parents-in-law got there that evening. She wondered if she should put it down in a bowl of water to be on the safe side. That can make it lose its taste, Maj-Britt says. Shall we, Nor's mother's wife said, and she nodded toward the bedroom. If truth be told, I just couldn't forget about the chicken, Nor's mother says, because if it didn't manage to thaw completely, then I'd need to turn the oven up a bit. That'd dry it out, Maj-Britt says. Nor's mother started to feel like the sex was dragging on, and it occurred to her that her wife was probably having a hard time leaving the slaughterhouse behind. Nor's mother knew from experience that the chicken wouldn't be tender, but maybe she could compensate with a splash of white wine, parsley, and some fresh herbs on top. Good plan, Maj-Britt says. At last they found a rhythm. Nor's mother's wife closed her eyes. Yes, Nor's mother thought, that's what I'll do. Yes, she yelled, yes. Didn't that give you an existential crisis, I ask Nor's mother. She shakes her head and says that her years of marriage with a wife who can't stand drama have trained her otherwise. If your emotional level rises above medium then she's out of there, Nor's mother says. You shouldn't go looking for problems that you don't have, Maj-Britt says, and she asks how it went with the chicken. It was perfect, Nor's mother says.

Dear Letterbox,

I'm a fifteen-year-old boy who has a hard time sleeping at night. The girl I'm in love with has just started a relationship with someone else from my class, and I'm devastated. I'm the type of person who thinks really deeply about things, and I have reached the conclusion that life is meaningless. I lie awake at night with my dark thoughts and my dread of the future. I have considered that I may be depressed, but I can't bring myself to talk to my doctor about it because I'm worried that he will put me in a psychiatric hospital.

Sincerely,

The Sleepless One

Dear Sleepless One,

You are fifteen years old, so you can't yet be a "type of person." Our frontal lobes don't fully develop until we are in our twenties, and until then we are by definition a little unpredictable. You have no idea what sleeplessness is until you've had a child, which I therefore strongly advise you against. It's sad that the girl you love isn't interested, but in a few years you won't even remember her name. In a way, that is even sadder, but you wouldn't understand that now. When things seem like too much to bear, it's important to ignore the future. Let go of the big picture and take life one minute at a time. You can't know when you'll get over your lovesickness, but, on the other hand, you *can* tell exactly when you want a cup of hot chocolate. Make things as simple and shortsighted as possible. Don't think that you want to have a good life, but that you want to have a few good days. When my driving lessons are feeling endless, it's partly because I'm always on my guard against the perils of the road. My driving instructor told me something simple but useful: the body always follows the eye. When you see a tree on the roadside, you don't turn your head and look at it, because then you'll drive into it. There is a widely held misconception that we should look our fears in the eye. The truth is that we should look in the other direction, otherwise we'll end up chasing after them. And don't be afraid of the doctor, it's the carefree segment of the population who ought to be in the psych ward, because anxiety is a fact of life for every thinking person. Our generation knows that planes can come crashing into buildings, that people can throw themselves into the sky. We understand that cells can divide in the body, that people can wear bombs under their clothes, that cars heading in the wrong direction suddenly appear on the freeways. All things must pass, but see this as a relief. Sweet Sleepless One, life is not an orderly event, but a fleeting and pointless movement around a dark room. And yet beauty can appear to us like something from another realm. A lovely poem, an unusual painting, a view that leaves us breathless. Your task is to use your time in the best possible way while you await death.

Warm regards,

The Letterbox

THROUGH THE WIDE windows of the dining hall I can see a pile of netting calmly rustling in the wind. Beside that are twenty-three pairs of waders splattered with various shades of brown. The outdoor education students have been fishing, and my son is licking a flounder. Little bits of breading are stuck to his tongue, which glimmers in the light of the ceiling fixture. Emma is sitting in the chair across from my boyfriend, and she contorts herself so that the maximum amount of her body is visible around her crop top. No, no, no, yells the organic nutrition teacher, and she runs over, weaving her way to the head of the table, where we've installed our son in his high chair. He could be strangled, she yells, and she clears away his plates. The organic nutrition teacher tells us about various children who have suffocated in an array of circumstances that could have been avoided. So you know three children who've died of suffocation, I say. It comes out that she has gotten it all from an article. But, the organic nutrition teacher says, that doesn't make them any less real, and she puts my son on her lap. He looks around for his fish fillet and then puts one of his fingers down into a bowl of remoulade and methodically smears the yellow substance onto his cheeks. I inform the organic nutrition teacher that we have a certified child of nature here before us. He can catch his own fish and he has a broad familiarity with small and medium-sized lugworms. One could go so far as to say that he could take over your job at the drop of a hat, I say. My boyfriend says that we have made a fully conscious choice not to teach our child that everything in the world is dangerous. There's no reason to play Russian roulette with his health, the organic nutrition teacher mumbles, but she says that it's up to us. After the meal the outdoor education students line up with the kitchen staff and receive the dining hall's general applause. Suddenly Emma screams and hoists our son out of the high chair. There is general tumult, the organic nutrition teacher runs out behind the head chef, who has five children and knows how to do the Heimlich maneuver. Not one of her facial muscles moves as she takes hold of our son, lays him on his stomach over her arm, and thumps him on the back. It goes by very quickly, and our son looks surprised when it's over. A little lake of vomit containing a white fishbone stares up at us from the checkered tablecloth, and the organic nutrition teacher consoles my boyfriend and me as we cry, our arms wrapped around one another.

WE ALWAYS THINK that this will pass, these nights of pacing the floor and singing lullaby versions of leftist folk songs about worker exploitation and surplus value. We've come up with a special way of starting a song at a loud, hysterical tempo, and gradually singing more slowly and quietly, until the melody dies out in a soft whisper. My son flings his arms around and laughs, but he starts to scream the second we stop singing. Although we do, in fact, like him, it's already apparent that he'll be the type of guy who stands as close as possible to the stage, his hair soaked with beer, yelling for an encore in a senseless delirium, thrilled, impatient, and incapable of waiting for anything. We dream of happy postcards from our son, an eager voice on Skype, photos of him standing on mountaintops or sitting on a beach surrounded by smiling young people. On the few occasions over the course of the spring when he has fallen asleep, we drink port wine and surf the internet. We look at images of tulip fields and canals that weave in unknown patterns through Amsterdam. We become happy, our cheeks start to glow. We imagine Heinekens and Gouda cheese, wild sex in cheap motels. Check the departures from Hamburg, my boyfriend says, and I think we both realize at the same time, as we are trying to find some reasonably priced train tickets in the year 2034, that we regard our son's childhood as a crisis situation, a carnival where we are dressed up in bizarre masks and dancing around to foreign rhythms. We had imagined that there would be no consequences to this dance, that in thirty years our son would catch up to us, and then the three of us would laugh together at the finish line, raise our long-stemmed glasses in a toast, and look back on his childhood like a wild party that you remember with great joy and partial memory loss. With a sudden and belated insight, we understand that our son will never catch up to us, that when he reaches our age, we will both be a little over sixty. We will be tired after all those years, maybe even more tired than we are now, although that's almost impossible to imagine. We will probably have bought an old farmhouse in Sweden, and we'll hope that our son might stop by with his family from time to time for a long weekend. We'll take his children out to see the elk, make bonfires by the lake, and count each other's mosquito bites the next morning. Our son and his partner will sleep peacefully in an annex, completely devoid of surplus value, and when they go home, we'll smile to one another and we'll feel like an old farmhouse ourselves. Someone will stuff the vacuum cleaner into its place in a closet, wipe the crumbs from the tables, bring the patio furniture back into the shed and fold it up. The shutters will be fastened, and one of us will make a final round, shut the door to each and every room, see the remains of a spiderweb, and not be bothered to remove it. Our shadows fall in the late afternoon sun, a lock clicks, a forgotten toy baby carriage hides behind the rosebush. We hear the sound of wheels on gravel, a car driving slowly away. We become a lonely old farmhouse that understands winter is on the way.

Lullaby for the Inconsolable
Elegy

Melody: Little Ida's Summer Song
(Lille Idas sommervise)
Composer: Georg Riedel, 1973

1 As the sun sets in the fjord
   the sky is like a painting so wide
   the earthworms crawl through the dirt
   and fall asleep to your cries
   as the waves crash along the shore
   the dunes huddle in their sandy bed
   we wander in circles and sing once more
   a little, desperate duet.

2 I think that when the time is ripe
   it's good to go off and see the world
   to travel all the way to the other side
   which is said to be so beautiful
   for while you see jungles and animals rare
   and go deeper and deeper into debt
   and live every day without a care
   then some time to ourselves we will get.

3 Yes, it is right outside our door
   with all of the lands you will see
   this beautiful and gruesome world
   so wonderful, strange, and crazy
   but suddenly you hear a cheering crowd
   and turn to look back from where you came
   where you see your parents so proud
   standing in the cold wind and rain.

4 A sheep in the twilight begins to bleat
   behind the thin curtain of night
   the cries of the rooks coming from the trees
   almost drown yours out, but not quite
   but finally the concert stops suddenly
   and silence makes its way in
   now you yawn and smile wearily
   and close your eyes once again.

The Land of Short Sentences

BETWEEN THE TWO lines, Parking Peter says, with an emphasis on between. We sit in his Audi by the municipal sports complex, two feet outside of the parking space. In the beginning I had trouble understanding what he was saying, but as it's turned out I've had plenty of time to decipher his dialect. Now you reverse backwards, Parking Peter says. Reverse, I say, it's just reverse. There's no telling what'll happen with you, says Parking Peter. I release the clutch and we nearly hit a parked bicycle. Even though we're reversing backwards, right is still right and left is still left, why can't women ever understand that, Parking Peter mumbles with a bitterness that, in a strange way, suits him. Hey now, I say, and I ask him if he really thinks you can generalize like that about one half of the world's population. Yes, Parking Peter says. We try another space. Turn, turn, turn, he yells, and he says that the only difference between driving forward and reversing is that you're not driving forward, but in reverse. Parking Peter asks if I'm right-left blind. I tell him that I wrote letters backwards when I was a child, and that it didn't stop until I was eleven. When I wrote my name it looked like characters from an Asian writing system. I think we need of one of these, Peter says, and he gives me a chocolate-covered caramel. I turn the wheel one and a half times and look over my shoulder. Parking Peter opens the door and checks the distance to the stripe. He says there's hope for the future, and we arrange for the next lesson. Do you want to pay under the table, he asks as he looks around for his calendar. I tell him that I'm a socialist and I pay my taxes gladly. Sounds expensive, Parking Peter says.

Dear Letterbox,

I am a young man who has recently become a father of twins. It's a great joy for me to have a family, and my wife is on almost all counts a fantastic person. But sometimes she can get mad at me for no apparent reason. I try to help out as much as possible and I don't think I shy away from my responsibilities. All the same, she looks at me every once in a while and says: Are you going to breastfeed them or should I? I've suggested that we transition to bottle feeding so that I can be more involved. Then she sighs and says that all nurses recommend breastmilk, as it prevents infections, asthma, and allergies. I don't understand what I'm doing wrong, do you?

Sincerely,

The Man

Dear Man,

My friend Frederik has a wife called Line. She had a very complicated birth that lasted over three days. Line had stopped speaking, but occasionally she twitched her head, as if she were surrounded by flies. In the middle of a storm of contractions, she suddenly heard Frederik ask a nurse for two ibuprofen. He had been up playing computer games all night, and when he was on the way to bed around three, Line's water broke. While Line was throwing up, she heard her husband saying to the midwife that he had probably been sitting wrong, that there was some tension in his neck. Line lifted herself up in the delivery tub, drops of water streaming down her massive body like small rivers. She crawled over the edge, hobbled naked out into the hallway, and grabbed the midwife, who was on her way to the medicine closet. For the first time since she went into labor, Line opened her mouth to say something that didn't resemble an unintelligible animal sound. If you give Frederik an ibuprofen, then I'll kill you, she said, as slowly and clearly as an actor reading an audiobook. The midwife, who was used to dealing with pregnant women, patted Line on the shoulder and started to unlock the closet. Line looked her in the eyes and put her arms around her neck. From a distance it looked like the beginning of an embrace, but Frederik was standing close by and he could see Line's fingers caressing the midwife's throat. The midwife looked at the alarm that hung on the opposite wall. Okay, she said, and she walked with Line back to the delivery room. I've discussed this with a number of my friends, and the opinions are divided. One can, of course, make the argument that Frederik should have had his ibuprofen, that one must distinguish between the two matters. The problem is just that this can be difficult to do. Dear Man, welcome to primal rage. What you have to understand is that this is a biological revolt against nature itself. You mustn't mistake it for common bitterness. We're dealing with a blind fury that has echoed throughout all time. What you are experiencing is not your wife's anger or her grandmother's, it is the deafening thunder of countless generations. It is the collective fear of being raped, the dizzying menstrual pains, the lonely childbirths, and the sense of constant ingratitude. It is no one's fault, but it's a burden we bear, and we can't always bear it in silence. Take heed of primal rage. Don't take it personally, but take it seriously.

Warm regards,

The Letterbox

IT'S THE EIGHTH of March, and I'm hosting a party to celebrate International Women's Day at Mylle's Café. I stand in the doorway, clad in my purple knitted sweater with fists and the female symbol across the chest. I'm sorry that I'm wearing a bra, Krisser says, and I'm sorry that I vote conservative, but thank you for letting me join. We look over at Emma, sitting at a table with some of the højskole students. She has dark circles under her eyes, and, in a group performance piece, the students have cut off most of one another's hair. They look like prisoners in a concentration camp, Krisser says, why do feminists always seem so angry. Take a glass of champagne, I say when people walk through the door, happy Women's Day. You can't call champagne champagne if it's not from Champagne, Krisser says. Asti is nice too, the principal says. No, Krisser says, Asti is a vulgar offense. Well, all right then, Mona says, and we toast. When I get drunk, it's always most clearly visible in my index finger. It shoots into the air every time I'm right about something, and it brooks no nonsense from anyone. I stumble after my lofty finger through the smoke of Mylle's Café. I'm gonna get my driver's license, I yell to Mona, nothing is impossible for the strong of heart. I tell the principal that she's shining, that her eyes beam like a thousand stars. Weep for me, weep, I whisper, it is Rome that's burning. Now now, says the principal. I actually like you, I whisper to Emma, because you're mad. Read Solanas, I say, read Bønnelycke, buy a revolver. Emma looks angry and flattered and she writes down the titles that I rattle off. I can tell that the organic nutrition teacher really has to pee and is trying to maneuver around Krisser, who has her trapped in a corner. They are talking about the højskole's green subjects, and Krisser has gotten mean-drunk. You're not an entrepreneur just because you have a little vegetable plot, she says to the organic nutrition teacher. You can't start up a business with a vegetable plot. The organic nutrition teacher explains the fundamental principles of permaculture, and Krisser groans. I look at the organic nutrition teacher and I think to myself that there's nothing more miserable than a tired idealist. She dreams of a world full of solar panels and edible insects, her cheeks glow red, and she burns for her cause. I'm about to lose my patience, Krisser says, and she rolls her eyes. Can you start up some shots, she yells, and tosses her wallet over to me. I catch it in the air just above Mona's ponytail. You have no idea what it means to run a hotel, Krisser says, looking intensely at the organic nutrition teacher, who shakes her head. The principal clinks two green bottles together and makes a speech about the women of Grundtvig's life. The nanny, the mother, and the wives. When I come back with ten shots of pomegranate vodka, Krisser has tears in her eyes and the organic nutrition teacher has her arm around her shoulder. Is it the chairs, I say. They both nod. When Krisser gets drunk, she always thinks back upon a regretted purchase for which she cannot forgive herself. The chairs are currently sitting in her lounge, and they look at her every morning in reproach. Their days are numbered, she mumbles, and she shows me photos of them from five different angles. The jukebox's music fades out, people's mouths move noiselessly up and down, and I gaze at Mona. I've always thought you were a divine beauty, I say to her. Mona gives me a glass of water and asks if we should go bang on some nails. The tree stump is in a back room, and Mona wins the game in five quick swings of the hammer. If truth be told, she practices at home in her garage when the driving students have been intolerable. You've got the chopping block all to yourself, little mama, Mona says, and she smiles at me. Why do you think everything is so hard for me, I ask. You're just a little bit, she says. A little bit what, I yell. Different, Mona says, and she passes me the hammer. A halo shines around her head, and I want to fall to my knees and propose to her in the middle of the oily concrete floor. Let's get you home, Krisser says, and she calls a taxi. A flawless method of contraception, I mumble. I suppose that depends who else is in the taxi, Krisser says. Cabbie-Connie hands me a plastic bag from the glove compartment and buckles my seatbelt. Before we turn down Fjordvejen, I can see Mona standing on a chair back in the bar. Who wants it, she yells. Velling, the whole bar roars, while the fjord lies in the darkness and listens.

WE'RE SITTING IN an old bunker down on the beach and looking out through a hole at the North Sea. Anders Agger has two little cakes from the farm store, and we watch the waves, which alternately pull back and roll in toward us like steady breathing. The beach foam is thick and looks like small sculptures made of soap bubbles dancing along the sand. He asks if I've made any progress, and if I've done my exercises. There was just one incident with the head chef, I say. She was going to teach me to make risotto, and we were cleaning the mushrooms with little brushes and chopping onions. Every eighth grain of rice should get stuck in your teeth, she said, watching me strictly as I grated parmesan cheese. I said that it would be wonderful if she lived at our house and could cook for us every evening. Nice, Anders Agger says, that acknowledges her expertise and expresses your gratitude. Thanks, I say. And the head chef agreed that that would be fun. Then you could also look after our son, I said, you're so good with children. Anders Agger writes something down in his little notebook, but I can't see what. Right, the head chef said, I guess so. You could get him to sleep in the evening, I said, and then afterwards you could sashay in to my boyfriend and me in the double bed and breathe some fresh air into our sex life. Anders Agger takes a sharp breath and tells me that I'm truly lucky not to have been born a man. The head chef picked up a mezzaluna knife and started to chop some flat-leaf parsley. It got totally quiet, and the rest of the kitchen staff stopped pouring, stirring, chopping, washing, kneading, and drying. There was something about the timing, I say, it almost seemed planned. You suffer from free-floating associations, Anders Agger says. With my mouth full of cake, I tell him that he's the only person who understands me. I try to get the whipped cream out of the tips of my hair. That may be taking it a little far, he says, but I do follow your logic. How did you get out of the situation, he asks with what seems to be true concern. Let's just settle on cooking and child-care, the head chef said decisively, and then everyone got back to work. You repeat your mistakes with an almost awe-inspiring determination, Anders Agger says. Count to ten before you speak, he says, shorter sentences and fewer metaphors. My lips are sealed, I mumble, but Anders Agger shakes his head and says that as long as there are words, there is hope.

I **SIT DOWN** in the passenger seat beside Malte, who, to his great dismay, got his driver's license last week. We're in front of my son's daycare and I'm trying to get his baby carriage into the car. The absolute worst part of motherhood is the requisite gear, I say to Malte. I hate any sort of equipment that has to be unrolled, folded up, or peeled apart. In general, anything that has to fit inside of another thing. It's a wonder I'm even capable of carrying out sexual intercourse, I say to the neighbor who is looking at me over his fence. I hate drying racks, sofa beds, trundle beds, reclining chairs, and Kinder eggs. High chairs, folding chairs, portable diaper changing stations. It follows that I have zero tolerance for baby carriages. The Emmaljunga stroller, people fawn, it's so easy to fold up. You just loosen the handles, a metal switch clicks, and ta-dah. But whenever I tug up on the two handles at precisely the same time, the baby carriage doesn't shudder in response like when other people do it. I count to ten, push the giant beast away from me, take a few steps back, and then approach it again. I give Emmaljunga a slap, because it has provoked me so. I try to get the metal switch to click, but when I carefully let go of one of the handles, the frame locks into place. I start to kick the baby carriage. At first an ever so slight tap on the wheel, so that a passerby might take it for a friendly gesture: good thing I have my baby carriage wheel. A kind of high five of the foot. Then I hammer my clenched fist down upon the canopy, cast it down onto the sidewalk, and try to keep my growling animal noises to a minimum. Maj-Britt opens the window and calls me with her gentle voice, the one she uses when two of the children want to play with the same doll. She yells for Bent, who comes running, and he picks up the toppled baby carriage. Maj-Britt passes a glass of water to me through the kitchen window. I discover that my face is dripping with sweat. I'm never like that with my son, I call up to Maj-Britt's face, which hovers over a potted plant in the window sill. Of course not, she says. Nor's mother parks her car and the children spring out. She starts to fold Emmaljunga up and says that this sort of thing never happens with an Odder stroller. She discovered the brand when they had their second child, and they've never used anything else since. The married couple who live across from Maj-Britt have come out to the street. They pick up my son's stuffed rabbit and brush it off. They had an Emmaljunga with their youngest child, and, along with Bent, they fold the frame together with the help of a sort of peg affixed to the bottom, which I had never noticed. I can barely breathe for my violent fantasies, because Emmaljunga, in a show of blatant favoritism, willingly allows itself to be folded together by the entire neighborhood, but fiendishly resists all attempts by the one who in fact owns it, namely me. I start to talk about my boyfriend. He believes that I engage in the habitual avoidance of practical things, I say, and he has made a rule that I have to learn to fold up the baby carriage myself. I'm sure your husband means well, the neighbor says. They aren't married, Bent says, and I slam the trunk shut. Now that Emmaljunga is out of sight, I can feel my rage shift its target. When I get home, I say, I'm going to kill my boyfriend. Nor's siblings look at me nervously. She doesn't really mean it, Nor's mother whispers. I make eye contact with the children and I nod my head. How will you do it, asks Nor's brother, who seems scared but also impressed. A shovel, I say, and the baby carriage is next. Go home and relax for a while, the neighbor says, you need a break from one another. It's not clear to me whether she is talking about my boyfriend or Emmaljunga. You have plenty of other talents, Maj-Britt yells to me before she shuts the window. My son waves to everyone from the backseat. Thanks for your help, I say to the little group. We want it in Velling, Nor's mother says with a smile.

Dear Letterbox,

I am an eighteen-and-a-half-year-old female with a lot on her mind. One of my teachers is an incredibly handsome man. He's tall and dark and he used to be a model. I'm so in love with him and I think that maybe he has the same feelings for me. At a school party we locked eyes across the beer keg, and he was the teacher on duty so I know he hadn't been drinking. A Whiter Shade of Pale was playing and I could barely breathe. I really wanted to dance with him but I felt like it would be inappropriate to ask. The next day I put up a link to the song on Facebook, and my teacher was the first one to like it. I'm going to graduate in half a year, should I wait until then to declare my love for him? Do you think he feels the same?

Sincerely,

Vanilla

Dear Vanilla,

Don't get me wrong, I understand the attraction. The beautiful, fantastical forbidden. That said, your letter seems to me to be a bit on the unrealistic side. Perhaps it's a human weakness, but I have zero tolerance for daydreamers. The way they float eight feet off the ground in their own world annoys me. For example, I'm quite fond of my neighbor Sebastian, and I like that he is easily inspired. But yesterday he sat in my living room for two hours and, eyes beaming, rhapsodized about the sustainable lifestyle. With a dreamy expression, he told me he was going to get chickens. Okay, I said, then get them. Sebastian was going to quit his job and get out of the rat race, as he put it. I could tell that he had read an article he shouldn't have read, that he had in all likelihood cut it out and hung it with magnets on the refrigerator door, that it had touched something within him, something dangerous and uncritical. He wanted to get off the hamster wheel and sell eggs up on the roadside, build an herb garden, and plant fruit trees. Parsley, rosemary, sage, he smiled, and I took a deep breath. You have two kids, I said, they need all kinds of things. There's more to life than things, Sebastian said, having gotten the completely incorrect impression that he was the one doing the educating. They need food, I said, clothes, Christmas presents. They need eggs and herbs, Sebastian chanted. He would feed the chickens every morning at dawn, stick his bare feet into a pair of sandals and toss a few handfuls of grain around the garden. It's the middle of

March, I said, it's way too cold. My words could not find their way into my neighbor's ears, which were stuffed with confused chickens. Dear Vanilla, if you want to go into the herb business, get in touch with a plant nursery. If you want a boyfriend, it shouldn't be the person who grades your final exam. When the music plays and the chickens cluck, one can get carried away, but remember, the orgasms aren't better just because something is forbidden. And you don't talk about your age in half years after you've graduated from preschool.

Warm regards,

The Letterbox

I COULD JUST picture it, Krisser says, explaining how she bought her summer house in Stauning last year when she was out on a walk one day. It spoke to me, Krisser says as she opens a bottle of white wine. In the following weeks, she was on hand to offer inspiration while her father-in-law fixed up the house according to her instructions. We make a very good team, she says, and she shows me the deck. I sit down in a lounge chair and look at the wooden floor that Karsten's father built. After we had known each other for a few months, Krisser started to be quiet. Silence can come over her like an unexpected gust of wind, and her eyes drift off. I bite my lower lip and think of Anders Agger. It's impossible for me to judge whether the situation is intensely awkward or entirely unremarkable. I start to panic and I write to him. Half a minute passes and my phone vibrates. She's just relaxed in your company, he answers. I light a cigarette and take a handful of chips. The crunching noise inside my head calms me down. Do you want to get matching tattoos, I ask. Maybe, Krisser says with a remote look on her face. It could be a seahorse, I say. Krisser asks if I think she could get the hotel drawn in miniature. She looks at her upper arm and says that the tattoo would probably be too wide if you included the extension. Friendship with Krisser can make me feel a little lovesick sometimes, and it's not the first time I've caught myself envying the hotel. I can tell that she's about to lose interest in our conversation, and her words dwindle to slight noises. You don't always need to talk, I think to myself, it's pleasant and relaxing to sit with a good friend and look out over the fjord. The children are sleeping, the sun is setting, the chips are crunching, the grass is growing. Our glasses are empty, and Krisser yawns gently. Look, a deer, I say, and I point over at some bushes at the edge of the garden. Where, Krisser says, standing up. It was just there, I say, and I lift my wineglass. Krisser sees them sometimes, walking around and nipping at the grass in the morning, and she and Vera wave to them. Did you know that a deer has four stomachs, I ask. No, Krisser says, and she becomes quiet again. What are you thinking about, I ask as nonchalantly as possible. I'm just spacing out, Krisser says. Are you tired, I say. Actually no, she says. Well I'd better get home, I say, and I get up. Why, Krisser asks, and she looks confused, as if I had interrupted something.

HOW LONG CAN two friends sit in silence, I shout to the principal, who is trimming her hedge. Fifteen minutes, she says, turning off her power trimmer, and a little longer if you're in a car. It's just different out here, the principal says as we sit down in her kitchen, there aren't so many people to choose from. Friendships form out of necessity, it's like a roadside ditch when you really have to pee: if you don't take what's available then you just have to hold it. Everyone needs witnesses and alibis, guests for their parties, company. The principal gives me a bag with a bow tied around it. Sebastian again, I ask. Like many of us, she didn't opt out in time, and now it's too late. Oh how lovely, the principal enthusiastically exclaimed the first time Sebastian proffered his homemade crispbread. It was made with spelt flour and five different grains, which he rolled himself, and Sebastian beamed and baked and doled it out. I'm crazy about crispbread, the principal enthused as she opened the package and took a big bite. Actually, I happen to hate having dry things in my mouth, she says. The crispbread was too hard, it crunched between her teeth, she could feel the crumbs getting stuck in her gums, and the principal wondered about her gold fillings. The many coarse grains exploded in her mouth, and she tried to use her tongue to push them away from her teeth. You can taste how healthy it is, the principal managed to say to Sebastian, her voice subdued by a mouthful of grains. Now there's crispbread every time they meet. She can't take a quiet stroll through the school's garden without Sebastian sticking his head out of his window and offering up another hard, square-shaped package. The week's provisions, he says as he smiles with all his big, pure heart. What do you all do with it, the principal asks. Straight to the birds, I say. There is a long list of names lying on her desk. Is this the marriage bureau, I ask, and she nods. The principal has a star system by which she rates every single person's companionability. Short-tempered but generous, is written next to the recently single hairstylist's name. Too soon, says the principal's husband as he washes a paintbrush, the corpse isn't even cold yet. Down the column I find my boyfriend's name, which has an arrow pointing to mine. There are five stars under his name, but I only have two. Well, well, I say. Being an only child automatically lowers your score, and your temperament comes into play a bit as well, she says. Sweet but stubborn, she has written under our names. You two are a closed case, it's just a necessary formality, says the principal.

Dear Letterbox,

I am a thirty-five-year-old woman who has been involuntarily single for a long time. I've tried everything, but it's impossible to find someone who meets my needs. I've considered going on *Married at First Sight*, but it might stress me out too much to be followed around by a film crew, because I'm a pretty private person. On the other hand, it would be painful to not go on the show and to watch my potential life partner go to someone else. I know that my one and only is out there, but how do I find him?

Sincerely,

The Searcher

Dear Picky One,

The terms we use to discuss dating are adopted from the language of consumerism. We speak of the single person's needs, desires, and requirements, which is bizarre, because the very thing we are longing for is a way out of the eternal me, me, me. The more you know about what you're looking for, the harder it is to find. We are all animals, and it is not possible for us to know ahead of time who is suitable for us, considering that reality isn't a bouquet of flowers you can arrange and set in the windowsill. Relinquish control and imagine that you are an open door leading out to the garden, a lounge chair is unfolded in the sun, a good book lying open in the grass. To meet a partner is to place yourself at the disposal of another person. Don't ask what your date can do for you, ask what you can do for your date. What most people believe they need is quite distinct from what they in fact desperately lack. The good news is that it's rather simple: If you are funny, you shouldn't look for someone else who is funny, but someone who likes to laugh. If you like to cook, then don't hunt for another chef, but find someone who is hungry. Dear Picky One, everyone has a lonely, dark room within. Imagine a pit at the bottom of the sea. We throw all sorts of things into it in an undignified fashion. Stamp collections, garden plots, backpacking trips, pets, alcohol, literature. In our weaker moments we begin to think that the pit is human shaped, a little jigsaw puzzle that's missing one piece. We look for the person who can fit it just right, who can drive the darkness away.

This is very sweet, but it is wrong. The darkness is our own, and it cannot be shared with anyone else. The one and only isn't someone else, it's you, and you are alone.

Warm regards,

The Letterbox

MY BOYFRIEND IS tired and hungover, and I can tell as soon as I start the conversation that he isn't in the mood for my life crisis. I feel trapped, I say, in a cage of babies and wind. It is early in the morning, and I can see that my boyfriend is wondering whether it would be acceptable to make himself coffee while I cry. His eyes flit around, he wants a cup of coffee so incredibly badly. He measures his path to the kitchen counter, where the coffee machine sits beside a tin of beans. For me there is only loneliness, while he has the spring, the højskole, and the tennis court waiting for him. He has plans with a colleague, and I can see him resisting the urge to look at his watch, how he is trying to study my face as he would a film screen, a storyline he will at some point have to summarize and review. He tries to stifle a yawn. Most women I know can yawn without opening their mouths, but he is not so professional. I can see him make up his mind, and he places two paper towels in front of me. He begins a sentence, backs slowly toward the counter, speaking all the while, and, as if by chance, he pours water into the kettle and grinds the beans. My boyfriend tells me it's completely all right to cry, and I suspect he is actually reminding himself that my tears are indeed allowed. I think the difference between us is his blind faith in consolation. The problem with my tears is that they blow by like rain showers, and, like episodes of 90210, they keep coming and coming. Just when you think it's impossible for there to be another season, that's when the reruns begin. The coffee drips, and I understand that all things have their limits. I know that my boyfriend is waiting, and when he is done waiting, then he will wait a little longer. Partly out of duty, but mostly out of love, although the two alternate and overlap a little. In all likelihood, we will reunite on the other side, him relieved, and me happier. But all the same, I know that the sequencing is essential, that there is always the possibility he will stop waiting before I stop crying.

CLENCH YOUR THIGHS, Krisser yells into my ear. We're sitting on a mechanical bull at an indoor amusement center called Baboon City, a little outside of Herning. It's a company excursion for the employees of Hotel Skjern, and Krisser insisted that I join. It will be really relaxed, she said when she knocked on my door in the morning , and you really need to get out of the house. She helped me into a T-shirt with the hotel's logo on the front. But why, I said, with the feeling that I was being punished for something I didn't do. Employee appreciation, Krisser said, and she slammed the car door shut. Krisser's name comes up often at The Main Office, and they are always hoping she won't be out on the road when their students are taking their driving tests. Why don't you ever use your turn signal, I asked Krisser. It's no one else's business where I'm going, Krisser said as she turned toward Herning. Her hurtling pace through this slow part of the world amuses me, but, in a way that I find moving, she can suddenly become completely still, unwavering as a decision. Sometimes she shows up out of nowhere right when I need her most, and she stays put. Now we're sitting here, close as can be, on the back of a bull. Just breathe and hold on tight, Krisser says. If this had come from anyone else then I would have assumed it was meant symbolically, a message to me about my life, but it's Krisser, and it means breathe and hold on tight. We bounce up and down in the saddle and cling to one another. Baboon City whirls by, faces dissolve and interchange, colors and plastic melt together, flickering like fears and dreams.

I DRIFT THROUGH the spring like a leaf in the wind, and every morning I sit on the dock down on the fjord. I watch the birds returning, the light-green ferns unfolding, and the cherry trees that blossom like an insult or a reminder. I see it as a kind of waiting, or a quiet protest. We don't talk about it, but Krisser comes by from time to time and sits beside me. I can't tell if she's looking for me or if she simply finds me. What's up, she says. Not much, I whisper.

Song for a Hopeless Spring
Psalm

Melody: It Smells Light Green of Grass
(Det dufter lysegrønt af græs)
Composer: Waldemar Åhlén, 1933

1 Through the hedges the wind does blow
   along empty suburban streets
   the year's first snowdrops begin to grow
   as they whisper of the deceased
   my sorrows increase
   and find no peace
   I stumble around and I yell
   alone among fools I dwell.

2 The lapwing returns home too soon
   the branches wave in the wind
   to whom I have not got a clue
   for the night is so barren
   my love is calm
   I carry on
   I hear the church bells ring
   as sorrowful as the spring.

3 I paddle ever so slowly away
   through a duct of tears
   the hedges are clipped under skies of grey
   the nightingale's cry fills my ears
   a final call
   a hope so small
   a light that must be on its way
   the coming summer days.

TRAFFIC IS A place where we all help one another, Parking Peter says, the other cars will make space for you. I ask how he can be sure of that, and I feel my pulse hammering through my body. We find ourselves on the Messe Motorway heading south around Herning. Everybody wants to get home for dinner, Parking Peter says. I am silent and trembling as we head down the on-ramp, and at last I shut my eyes and put my blinker on. Don't think of the other drivers as enemies, Parking Peter says, most of them are just friendly people on their way from point A to point B. That's important to remember, he says, although he's also seen drivers who undergo a personality change when they get behind the wheel. Courteous people who happily let others in front of them in the line at the grocery store, but who are almost ready to kill out on the road if the car ahead of them is driving too slowly. Because the automobile is a private space that moves through the public arena, people more easily feel that their boundaries have been crossed. Parking Peter says that the same can be said for the internet. Because people can't see one another's faces, they forget that there are living people sitting behind the keyboards and communicating with them. I ask him what his greatest weakness is as a driver. Speed, Parking Peter says. Throughout the years he's only gotten a single ticket, but every once in a while he takes a solo trip to Germany. What do you do, I ask. Put the pedal to the metal, Parking Peter says, there's no speed limit on the highways there. If there's something I like about Peter, it's that he always answers my questions as if it's a part of his job. For me, the car is like a confession booth, and I tell everything that I have thought and felt since I last sat there. Peter has come to receive my confessions with an astonishing sense of calm. While speaking, I've stopped pressing the gas pedal, and Parking Peter points at my left foot. Let's pass it, he says, after we've been driving behind a big eighteen-wheeler for a few minutes. My hands shake, and I signal and stare blindly into the rearview mirror. Not out on the shoulder, Peter yells, use the left lane. Sorry, I say, and I give him a quick look. In the midst of his patience sits a wolf staring out through his eyes, and it occurs to me that it's only possible to project that level of calmness if you can also explode. This particular form of restraint cannot be won without a fight, you put it on like a windbreaker because you know that it's going to be blustery. I've steadily stirred up a long-simmering aggravation within him, a breathless curiosity, a jumble of students and friends, cars and old spare parts. Will you miss me if I get my driver's license one day, I ask. I will, Parking Peter says, you can get used to anything.

ANDERS AGGER ASKS if there is any news from the conversational battlefield. We're sitting in his living room drinking coffee, and I tell him about my ups and downs on the front lines. He thinks I should work on establishing neutral relationships. You don't need to be close to everyone, he says, sometimes it's fine for people to maintain boundaries between them. You yourself made a documentary series called *From Within*, I say, and you have a television station to help you arrange interviews, not everyone has the same advantages. All the same, Anders Agger says, you also have to think for yourself. He passes me a bowl of cookies. Homemade, I ask. Store-bought, Anders Agger replies. I help him wrap prizes for the Ringkøbing soccer club's bingo night, and the floor is strewn with paper and ribbons. Do you have time for this sort of thing, I ask. Anders Agger shakes his head and explains that he has a hard time saying no. It's the windmills, he says. When Anders Agger walks in his garden, he can hear the sound of the wings spinning. Yes, yes, yes, yes, they whisper across the lawn and the redcurrant bushes. It's like it's contagious, he says, put me in front of an altar and I'd be married within an hour. I'm well acquainted with this, I say as I cut a piece of wrapping paper off the roll, but it must be resisted. My face and my body are one big resounding yes. When I walk down Strøget in Copenhagen, I am surrounded by homeless people, street musicians, and hungry birds. They can tell that I can't say no. I'm a member of everything you can be a member of in Denmark. It's not because I'm particularly socially conscious, I just get too easily entangled in other people's problems. I gaze back at the aggressive donation collectors with my sewage-colored eyes and I can picture it all as they expound upon the world's problems. A frightened panda with a mouthful of bamboo. The decimation of rainforests, endangered species, starving war refugees, battered women. Children's aid organizations in need of resources, sad Muslims in need of a mosque, entire feature films project onto my retinas with just one introductory sentence. Yes, I shout, yes, of course I'll help, and the fundraiser looks back in disbelief, because she hasn't yet reached the high point in her monologue, she's only just begun, and now she feels an unexpected disappointment. She likes to tell herself that she is tired of her script, but now that I've taken it away from her, she raises her eyebrows in annoyance. She drops the act, but I'm already hooked, and, deeply moved, I sign whatever it is in the name of justice. At a certain point, my bank forced me to unsubscribe from several organizations, I say to Anders Agger. They didn't want to finance my role in world peace, as my advisor put it. I had to call round to a number of unsympathetic, fiery souls, but it actually wasn't as bad as I had thought it would be. I was well prepared, I gave my apologies and regrets and said I would be back the very moment that I became rich. You need to learn a new word, Anders Agger says. The wonderful, transformational word, *yeaoo*. At first you say yes, as usual, but then, after a short while, your yes almost imperceptibly turns into a no. You've got to keep your promises, Anders Agger says, and he ties a bow around one of the gifts. That's a luxury reserved for the naysayers, I say, the rest of us have to be more pragmatic, otherwise we can't do anything but serve the needs of a demanding world. Are you with me, I ask. Yeaoo,

Anders Agger mumbles. Louder, I yell, and I point to the mountain of not-yet-wrapped gifts. Yeaoo, he says, and we open the door to his garden. Yeaoo, we howl in unison, running between tulips and strawberry bushes, yeaoo, yeaoo, yeaoo. Wasn't that nice, I say. Yes, Anders Agger says, and I follow his gaze up to the clouds rolling across the sky.

Dear Letterbox,

I'm writing to ask your advice concerning my ex-girlfriend. We have lived together for years, but we decided to part ways after realizing that our dreams for the future are incompatible. There is no direct animosity between us, and for practical reasons we have to keep living together for a few more months, but I get angry every day when I see her. Since we made our decision, it's like I can't see anything good in her, even though I know that she's a wonderful person. Everything I value in her has disappeared and is replaced with a contempt that is both disrespectful and out of proportion. We need to divide our possessions and uncouple our lives in a reasonable way, so avoiding all communication is not an option. We are both in our fifties and we don't have any kids together. How should I deal with my negative feelings?

All the best,

The Bitter One

Dear Bitter One,

Just as one train can block your view of another, anger often hides other feelings, which, as a rule, are hunger, sorrow, or fear. Perhaps you are just furious with your ex-girlfriend because something has vanished from your life. It can be compared with losing your child in the grocery store. When you find them again, you scream at them out of pure love. Personally, when I meet people I've once loved, my anger is just an act it is impossible to maintain. If I let it go for one moment, the rage is transformed into an unbroken love that mercilessly lives on, and that can rouse itself at any moment. Dear Bitter One, within the labyrinth of anger lies the garden of sorrow, and you should visit it as necessary.

Warm regards,

The Letterbox

MY BOYFRIEND HAS invited the students he advises over for hot chocolate, and the twelve of them are huddled outside our door in one big clump. Some of them have their arms around one another, others are holding hands, but every one of them is smiling, as if there were something ritualistic about the threshold they are about to pass through. In little groups, they will sit and talk about what they felt when they arrived at the højskole, what they're feeling now, and what they've felt in between. They give him a bouquet of flowers and tell him we have a nice place. They look trustingly at my boyfriend and me, the way you look at adult people, and I think that it's only a matter of time until we are exposed. A couple of years ago, my boyfriend and I held a party that went a little off the rails. We had driven around Poland with some friends that summer, and we came home with five different kinds of vodka. We made a blind taste test, and the evening progressed in a chaotic direction. The neighbors knocked on our door because they didn't want to listen to Judas Priest and our friend Troels fell asleep in the bathroom with his blindfold on. My boyfriend and I passed out cold after having drawn a penis on Troels's cheek pointing toward his lips. The next evening we were lying on the sofa, watching the evening news with awe-inspiring hangovers. Suddenly Troels popped up on the screen, because there was a new research project on alcohol drinking among young people, and as a sociologist he was giving a comment. There is a lack of oversight in the area, Troels said, and he opined that the results were worrying. If you looked closely, you could see an oval shadow on the right side of his face, but for the unwitting it could easily have been mistaken for beard stubble. Otherwise he was perfectly polished, his tie sitting correctly, and this is how I often feel. My boyfriend is talking about the school's alcohol policy on field trips. He says that when you visit another country, there is no reason to spend half your time with a hangover. The point is to get something out of the days, my boyfriend says. The students want to know if there are rules about how much they can drink. No, I say. But it's not forbidden to use your head, my boyfriend says, and the students laugh. Well, I say, sometimes you have to just go with your instincts. You don't ask for permission to lose control, where's your sense of rebellion, I ask, don't you have any initiative. My boyfriend advises them to bring appropriate footwear. If I may be a little direct, I say, it's my opinion that you should have more sex and stop thinking so much. Only if that's what you want, my boyfriend says, it's also completely fine to say no. I say that it's a mistake to believe that one's sexual escapades need to reflect one's human values. I myself have broad tastes, and it makes things easier, I say, it's important to be open to the world. The students nod with serious expressions. And now we'll say thank you to our commentator, says my boyfriend, who thinks that I should reserve my advice for people who have written me and asked for it.

I SIT IN Sebastian's cargo bike and eat popcorn while he hums fragments of a melody he hasn't quite got a hold of yet. We are alone with our children for the whole week because the højskole is on a trip to Hungary. Is that wise, my mother asks through the telephone. Imagine if a student seduces him, she says, you hear about that kind of thing. I roll my eyes at Sebastian. My mother talks about how many parties there are at højskoles and how alcohol can incapacitate even the highest moral characters. But of course he doesn't exactly like them young, my mother says, you being four years older. Exactly, I say. So it'll probably be a colleague, my mother says, which isn't quite as bad, but still impractical given that you live at his place of employment. I say that the principal keeps her flock under control, and I can hear my mother nodding. An incredibly beautiful woman, she says, and some men out there gravitate to women who could be their mothers. I make it clear that my boyfriend and I are doing just fine. According to my mother, I'm completely obsessed with my boyfriend and always have been, but she concedes that he has feelings for me as well. Maj-Britt squints when we park outside of her garden. She approaches us slowly, with her eyes trained on Sebastian's stomach. It's protruding, Maj-Britt says gravely, and she pulls the arms of his jacket up. Normally it is almost impossible for her to lose her composure, but Maj-Britt admits she has a short fuse when it comes to shoddy handiwork. With her index finger, she follows the stitching that meanders across Sebastian's upper body. She tugs at the green fabric between the zipper and lining and sighs loudly. God help us, Maj-Britt says, and her exaggeration stirs an unexpected glee within me. What kind of a pervert are you, I whisper to Sebastian when Maj-Britt goes inside to get her sewing kit, protruding outside of a daycare. Maj-Britt holds some threads in different shades of green up to Sebastian's sleeves. Which tailor did you use, she asks, was it Bride, Party, and Sew. Sebastian can't remember, and Maj-Britt pulls the jacket off him as if he were one of the children in her daycare. Bent will bring it by tonight, she says, and she takes it to the kitchen. Sebastian studies a plastic container of oatmeal and asks if Maj-Britt rolled it herself. No, she says, as she begins to thread a needle. Sebastian sits down at the kitchen bench and talks about crispbread while Maj-Britt carefully removes his zipper and sews it back on again. Mooo, yells my son, and he runs toward me. There's no way this is still normal, I say. It is, Maj-Britt says. I put jackets on our two certified children of nature while Sebastian expounds upon the difference between flour made with and without grains. Now we've all been put through the mill, Maj-Britt says.

Dear Letterbox,

I'm a woman who in the past year has started to receive my pension, and along with it I've gotten a new existence with much more time on my hands. I've been using it to arrange get-togethers with the neighbors at our summer house. I put a lot of effort into preparing the food and decorating with flowers and lanterns. I have the impression that people enjoy themselves, but they rarely extend invitations back to me. I'm worried that I may have misinterpreted our relationship as neighbors, and that the other summerhouse owners see me as an oddball who can't take a hint. Should I cancel the barbeque I've been thinking about, or just carry on undaunted?

Sincerely,

Regitze

Dear Regitze,

Allow me to lift the curtain of your confusion. Because you are a generous and energetic person, you don't understand how we mere mortals operate. A few years ago, my boyfriend and I decided to throw a harvest feast. Naturally, the idea had occurred to us at a different party, where, after a lot of beer, we sat out in the bright summer night, and the world felt open and boundless. We're gonna have a party, we shouted to one another, and we invited everyone we knew. Then the darkness came creeping in. Every time a practical question comes up, a debilitating weariness inflicts my boyfriend and me. Something in us dies every time we have to attend to something concrete. We've moved a couple of times over the course of our relationship, and it always goes something like this: We talk about it for a few months. We fight a little, apologize to each other, agree that stress is to blame. Then we curl up in a fetal position while our parents come and box up our books and bag up our clothes and make sure we get something to eat. Thank you, we whisper, and we fight our way through the government website where we can officially change our address. After our parents have driven all our moving boxes to our new home and installed the lights and painted, my boyfriend and I are totally exhausted and we promise ourselves that we're never going to move again. Our friend Mathias suggested we could hold the harvest feast at his place, but by then we had become stubborn. That's not going to happen, my boyfriend said, and I shook my head. In the week leading up to the feast, torn pieces of paper were scattered around our apartment. These notes said beer, chips, dip. Later, more notes were written, with question marks after the words. Barbeque. Billy Holiday. Dill. We made shopping lists and checklists and guest lists, then got rid of them and wrote new ones, added and erased. Optimistic fantasies of cancellations and sudden illnesses proliferated and became a regular part of our days. Maybe we'll get food poisoning on the night before the party, I said. Maybe we'll need to renovate because of dangerously corroded pipes, my boyfriend said. We wanted so badly to find a shortcut to the day after the party, to simply jump right over it and onto the memories. It was the Muslims who saved us in the end. We had a direct view of a mosque, and it inspired us to investigate whether our feast fell during the month of Ramadan. It was close enough, and we wrote an apologetic email to our friends explaining we didn't want to insult a religious ritual with our senseless drinking. It would send a bad signal to the neighborhood if those who were fasting became involuntary witnesses to our excesses. Our sweet, left-wing friends were understanding, and some even went so far as to praise our solidarity. Dear Regitze, the gatherings that you can throw together in blink of an eye can take the life out of others. It's a gift to be practically inclined, and you must never take it for granted. Up with the lanterns, out with the grill, and let the drinks flow till the morning sun dances in your eyes.

Warm regards,

The Letterbox

PARKING PETER AND I sit in his Audi in front of the police station. We are nervous and tense because we're on the way to my driving test, and if he weren't from West Jutland I believe he would have held my hand. I find my glasses in my bag and lean back in the seat. Parking Peter wants to give me one last bit of advice, and he starts talking about *The Godfather*, which he watches every year at Christmas. There's a specific scene where the gangsters are getting rid of a body and want it to seem like a normal cause of death. Make it look like a traffic accident, the gangster boss says to his underlings. Of course, that's not what you should do, says Parking Peter, but think about putting makeup on a corpse, you want it to look natural. Do you see what I mean, he asks. The road-test administrator approaches, and we get out of the car. He flips through my driving records in confusion, and looks at Parking Peter. Eighty-seven lessons, he says. That's right, says Parking Peter, but she can do something which neither of us are capable of. He explains that I gave birth to a child between my driving lessons, and that's got to count for something, all things considered. And zero mistakes in her written test, Peter says, as if he's trying to sell me. Because I'm nervous, I didn't eat before the test, and I'm beside myself with hunger. My passion for food always flares up in a wild and aggressive fashion when I'm menstruating. The road-test administrator is called Ole, and he says that it's up to me whether we talk or not, and that I shouldn't feel pressured to. I prefer silence, I say, so I can concentrate on my driving. Ole says he understands, and that he thinks it's a wise choice. We drive toward Grønnegade, and he clears his throat several times in quick succession. I'm supposed to yield at the intersection, one of the few to be found amidst the roundabouts of Ringkøbing, and I brake hard. I'm really hungry, I say as we drive by The Steak on Vester Strandgade. I've stopped eating beef, but the world's CO_2 emissions become less important to me when I'm hungry. What's one steak in the grand scheme of things, I say, and Ole is with me all the way on that. While we talk, Ringkøbing glides by like an ignored TV advertisement. I signal, wait, look in the mirror, check over my shoulder, but all I can see are phantom steaks. Ole's wife loves salad and tarts, steak is a rare luxury. It would be a different story if you'd married me, I say, I can guarantee you that. I talk about making béarnaise sauce from scratch with tarragon from the garden and lots of butter. He guides us into an industrial area and asks me to back around a corner. I try three times, but I wind up either on the curb or way out in the street. Ole looks disappointed at first, then a little sad, and, on the final attempt, outright suicidal. Can you at least stay in your own lane, he asks, and he glances at his watch. We drive back in silence. When we stop in front of the police station, he looks at me. You can have your license, he says, but promise me that you'll only drive forward. I embrace him, and Ole says: There, there. When I get out of the car, a little group is waiting. The surfer is biting his nails, Mona is chain-smoking with Malte, and Parking Peter is smiling at me. I wave the little white note that comprises my temporary driver's license, and everyone starts to clap. I reach out my right hand toward the surfer, and he gives me a high five. Mona comes up beside Parking Peter. This is a milestone in your career, she says, and the two shake hands.

Krisser parks her Mercedes in front of the police station and uncorks a bottle of champagne. It makes a loud pop, and everyone yells hurrah. In you go, Krisser says, as she sticks a cigar between my lips.

SEBASTIAN IS PACKING up his guitar. Soon we'll take the stage at Velling's midsummer festival, and we've just run through our repertoire. Will you be protruding at home this weekend, I ask, and Sebastian sighs. He says that they are having a hard time finding the spark amid their busy lives, but there will be plenty of time for protrusions when he and his wife retire. I introduce Sebastian to the slap system, which my boyfriend and I have developed. For a while the only thing we talked about were the wet wipes we used, because we were changing diapers all the time. Why was it that the top wet wipe in the pack was always almost dried out. Was it because we were just bad at sealing the lid all the way, or was the brand of wet wipes that we used on the dry end of the wet-wipe spectrum. It raised a long series of questions. Were our wet wipes wet enough, or could you get wet wipes that were wetter. And how wet should a wipe be in order to be classified as a wet wipe. We tried out different kinds, gave one another reports on the day's wet wipes, felt them with our hands, and looked to one another with the expressions of critical consumers. At first we were a little ironic about it, because we could hear the way we were talking. We laughed and spoke in funny voices when we talked about wet wipes. Slowly, seriousness took over, and we spoke in academic tones. We began to rank the wet wipes with stars, we wrote down their scores and hung the list up on the refrigerator. When we stopped feeling like detectives, we turned into robots. We still talked about wet wipes, but it was completely mechanical, and neither of us even realized it. It was the principal who informed us bluntly that it seemed unhealthy. We protested, but it was purely pro forma, because we knew that she was right, that wet wipes had become a clanging instrument within our daily lives, which we went around rattling without stopping to ask whether either of us liked the way it sounded. It was a shock to discover that wet wipes were symptomatic of a far more dangerous conversational sickness, I say. We had to acknowledge that, in the majority of the interactions we were having, neither of us in fact wanted to take part. Why isn't he sleeping, has he had enough to eat, is he crying or just whining, does he have a stomach ache. Our son looked at us with his big eyes, but he never said anything. Sometimes he smiled at us, other times he threw up or pooped his green poop, but he revealed nothing. I'm not saying that you should never talk about practical things, I say, that's absolutely necessary. You can also speak at length about it, but it should be a choice that you've made. Otherwise your conversations will be invaded by phantom children. They will spread throughout your home, I say, looking gravely at Sebastian. They'll plop down on your sofa and eat your popcorn, sit on your kitchen counter and talk incessantly while you make your dinner, adopting the tones of radio hosts and television news anchors. They will lie between you in your double bed, I whisper, and sing you to sleep, and your eyelids will slam shut out of pure and simple boredom. Your home and your thoughts will become containers of anxiety, pureed vegetables, porridge, milk, urine. So, I say, talk about the things you need to do while you are doing them. Don't let them fester. If the baby is hungry, talk about food. While you change diapers, talk about shit. When you sleep, talk about sleep. But if you don't follow the rules, then you get a slap, I say, and I hit myself on the cheek with the palm of my hand. And it's not just for fun, I say, lifting my index finger. You have to give yourselves the hardest slaps you can, white handprints and blood-red cheeks, rattling jaws, and a double slap when things go entirely wrong. The spark is something you've got to tend to, and you don't do it with sex, but with language. Physical intercourse is a form of etiquette that demands nothing but functional sexual organs. A good conversation, on the other hand, requires both imagination and intimacy. Do your best, I say. It's so easy lose control of your vocabulary, so try to avoid words like tater tots, cake pops, and carrot sticks. A shared confidence is the most beautiful thing you can give your lover, the trust inherent in a long anecdote. Think of language as a complex sex game, I say, hit yourselves and hit each other. Doesn't it hurt, Sebastian asks. Yes, I say, but that's the point. I myself have gotten cuddling slaps, nursing slaps, and diaper slaps. Now we don't ever talk about our child, I say. Try it, and nothing will stand in the way of your protrusion.

AS I BIKE over the viaduct on the way to Velling, it's as if nature is putting on a show for me. The horizon is like a sideways exclamation point atop the sea, which casts itself into my eyes, and the trees lean up against one another like a tribe of dancers. Maj-Britt comes running when she hears me at the door. I was just about to call you, she says, sounding shaken. She has my son in her arms. What does the sheep say, Maj-Britt asks, and she looks just as proud as my son when he smiles shyly and whispers: Baaah. What did you say, I shout, and I swing him in the air. Baaah, my son repeats as we spin dizzily around. We laugh and baaah all the way home. When we get to the gravel driveway I yell for my boyfriend, who comes running out. Our son understands that he is the star, and pauses theatrically when I point to him. Baaah, he says solemnly. My boyfriend grabs my hand. Baaah, we say in unison. We look at our son, enchanted by his journey within the realm of vowel sounds. Baaah, our son repeats, now forceful and decisive, and my pride stumbles vaguely into the future. I imagine lovesick teenagers coming to blows over his affection, sports matches in which he will play a central role in the victory. I know that he will spread light wherever he goes, make the days livelier, the world more beautiful, and its people better. Baaah, says my son.

Dear Letterbox,

I'm writing with a dilemma I hope you can help me with. After having been happily married for sixteen years, I have begun to have romantic thoughts about one of my neighbors. After a gathering with mutual friends, we became friends on Facebook and we started writing one another. It hasn't come to outright infidelity, but there is a spark between us that won't burn out. I am deeply grateful for my wife and especially my children, but I'm blinded by my love. Do you think it will pass, or should I get a divorce?

Sincerely,

The Despairing One

Dear Despairing One,

What a mess. Let me tell you about my good friend
Maria. Many years ago, she was on a cycling holiday
with her boyfriend. She was happy that summer, and
she wanted to buy ice-cream cones, one for herself and
one for Rasmus. She was standing at an ice-cream truck
and looking at the flavors. Chocolate, vanilla, mint,
banana. She considered the toppings and the sprinkles
and looked up at the ice-cream man. Then she froze.
There was something about his eyes, something about
his expression. They started talking, and she forgot all
about the chocolate, the vanilla, the mint, and the
banana. They talked and talked as the line grew longer,
until the people at the end were getting hit by the waves
down on the beach. Later on, Maria had no idea what
they had talked about, it was like their faces had talked
to one another in another language, she only remem-
bered the sounds and the laughter. Afterward, she went
back to their campsite by the Baltic Sea, confused, with
two ice-cream cones in her outstretched hands. They
were melting by the time she found Rasmus, and he
smiled and said, that took you a while. Maria nodded
and wanted to cry. She was ready to run back to the ice-
cream man and throw everything away in one grand
gesture. Little drops of ice cream dripped from Rasmus's chin, and Maria sat on a bench and ate hers in big
bites. Then they sent postcards to their friends and
took photos of one another as they laughed. A few days
later, they traveled home. That was eleven years ago.
Rasmus and Maria are happily married today and are

expecting twins. All the same, the ice-cream man still pops up in Maria's thoughts. This isn't supposed to be about me, and certainly not about Maria, but what I'm trying to explain is that we all have an ice-cream man. They can show up in various guises and in the most unexpected places. Suddenly they are standing there in the costume of a melancholy doctor, swabbing your throat, or a seasonal worker at your farmers' market. What can I do for you, they ask with a smile, and you have an urge to say: Everything. Let me see your beautiful soul, and give your darkness to me. You are trapped on an island, there is water all around you, and you know it's only a fata morgana you're seeing, an acid trip, a phantasmagorically long joint. All the same, you have the feeling that it's the summer itself you are about to miss out on, a magical ice cream that will never melt. Dear Despairing One, everyone has that phone number they lost one windy night on the way home from town, everyone has felt the pangs of bad timing like a stinging slap. Some of us are haunted by ice-cream men, we hide from them, hoping they'll drift by. Love can appear out of nowhere, and although it can be impractical, it's not dangerous. Contrary to what most people think, situations like yours don't arise out of boredom, but rather a trembling jubilation. It is summer, the days are long, the nights are bright. We need our infatuations, and every single time desire hits me like a cloudburst, that lusty madness that could love anyone at all, it is, above all, a muddled expression of joy that the world exists.

Warm regards,

The Letterbox

IT'S POURING RAIN when I see Emma on the road home from the grocery store. She's walking toward me in something that resembles a long, black cape, and she is carrying three raspberry roulades in her hands. I pull over and open the door. It won't do to let the roulades get wet, I yell. She gets into the car and says that she feels like I have a problem with her personality. No, I say, my heart goes out to even the most difficult children. Emma looks at me with her eyes as black as paint and it makes me miss my own rage, which has been replaced by a resentful annoyance toward things of lesser significance. Emma, I say, even though we're in love with the same person, we don't have to be mortal enemies. Emma opens her backpack and passes me a piece of gum. For your own sake, she says. I turn into the højskole's parking lot and turn the car engine off. Emma says that she and my boyfriend actually have crazy good chemistry. I don't doubt that one bit, I say, but remember that he's getting paid to spend time with you. Emma asks if we have a monogamous relationship, because she thinks that's old-fashioned and personally she would feel restricted. Welcome to love, I say. She says that there's solid evidence that you stagnate as an individual if you don't switch partners at minimum every five years. I say that I value people who fearlessly question social norms, that I admire their ambition and curiosity. But don't come and tell me that a lifelong love relationship isn't the most crazy and radical idea that a person can cast themselves into. It's experimental, intense, and recklessly hopeful. You're up against time itself, I say, invisible but appreciable changes through the years, premises that shift like the wind. It's a balancing act, a miracle, when two people are able to love one another over the course of a lifetime. Or maybe it's just a little unimaginative, Emma says. A little group of students are smoking in front of the main entrance while they look out at the rain. What about Malte, I ask. He's in love with Mona, Emma mumbles. We're all in love with Mona, I say, it's a virus in Velling. Get in the game, I say, but get into a game you can win.

Song for a Sunless Summer
Midsummer Song

Melody: Now the Earth and Heaven Are Still
(Nu er jord og himmel stille)
Composer: Carl Michaël Bellman, 1791

1 As I lie silently dreaming
here on virtue's narrow path
the grass is growing beneath me
and the years of my youth do pass
the soldiers of the summer
are marching through my soul
my hunger sated with a wafer
like a sinner no longer bold.

2 The sharp eyes of the osprey
look down on me with scorn
my heart it beats so wildly
as the bright night turns to morn
my heart is battered badly
when cupid's arrows fly
like a dartboard he aims at me
and he always hits bullseye.

3 Let the old flames burn once more
   like a final, soft farewell
   a thousand fires on Denmark's shores
   extinguishing themselves
   but some dreams must live on
   though reality may grieve
   restless hearts must meet the dawn
   when the bright night takes its leave.

WE'RE ON THE way to the supermarket, and the little red stripe on the gas meter is heading toward zero. Let's get better at pumping the gas so we don't suddenly wind up with an empty tank, my boyfriend says, looking at me. He has a fear of being poorly provisioned, so every single time he sees a gas station, he fills the tank, greedily and full of joy. Because he's become the gas pumper in the relationship, I never even make it to the station, and if the stripe approaches the red zone, I rest assured that it will all be fine. As an only child and a self-assured individualist, it was hard for me in the beginning. Although I am perversely fascinated by communities, I've had to learn to be a we. Right from the beginning of our relationship my boyfriend said we instead of you, which both confused and annoyed me. Can we try to get out the door faster, he asked. Can we take it easy with the chili peppers. For a conniving person such as myself, it's hard to understand people if they don't have a hidden agenda, and for a long time I thought it was a conscious rhetorical trick. The first summer my boyfriend and I were together, we were invited to a wedding. We had spent the entire morning helping my father paint his living room, and we packed our nice clothes in a blue messenger bag because we were planning to check in to the hotel and take a quick shower before the ceremony. We were in high spirits on the bus and we swung the bag around. We'd better be careful so the wine bottles don't break, my boyfriend said sweetly, with a nervous expression. I swung the bag again, perhaps a bit more violently than before. Catch, I said, throwing the bag to him, as we waited at a deserted small-town train station. The three bottles of red wine meant for the bridal couple distributed themselves over a white shirt, a suit, and a bright summer dress. We arrived to the wedding party giftless and in paint-flecked work clothes, and the bride's mother ended up driving us to the nearest town where we bought new outfits at a discount department store. Later, as we stood in the garden for the welcome drink, I heard my boyfriend telling the story. It's so typical of us, he lied, who carries three bottles of wine around in a soft bag. I realized right then that there is a winding road out of loneliness. So I make my voice a little deeper and serious-sounding, the way I know he likes it. Yes, I say, let's definitely be better at filling the tank in time.

Dear Letterbox,

We have to tell you that we love your responses, and that your advice column has a cult following among our group of friends. We are a young couple who, after many obstacles, have finally gotten together. We met in a medium-sized high school, and, as one of us is an employee and the other an attendee, it's been a challenge to hide such strong feelings during the school day. There are six weeks until the final exam. What should we do?

Sincerely,

The Secret Lovers

PS What you wrote about orgasms isn't true.

Dear Advisor and Vanilla,

If you really want to keep a secret then you shouldn't ask for advice from a publicly distributed newspaper. But I appreciate your praise, I've always wanted to have a cult. In a way, I'm happy to have played a role in your love story, but to be frank, it's bad publicity for my otherwise exemplary advice column that you all haven't followed my advice. But anyway. It would be advantageous for you to keep the school's leadership in the dark, as not everyone would look kindly upon your relationship. I happen to live at a højskole, and in the employee contract it says in black and white that the employees may not have sexual relations with the students, unless it's a case of true love. If an official guideline can function as a portrait, then this gives a finely drawn picture of the principal's innocent blue eyes, as well as the kind of trust that holds both højskoles and countries together. I think that this should be the rule in all academic settings. Dear Advisor and Vanilla, since the two of you won't listen to me, I'll just say that I hope there's been sex on the teacher's desk and sky-high grades. There ought to be some advantages. Look forward to the summer vacation, enjoy your drama, and dance with me in your dreams.

Warm regards,

The Letterbox

THE SUN IS shining into the kitchen when I come in to my son's daycare. Soon we'll have to go out and buy them caps, Maj-Britt says. She's ironing patches onto a pile of little green shirts. A few days ago we were sent home with a form where we had to put a cross by the symbol we wanted on the T-shirt. You could choose different pictures of plants and animals. It's the municipality, May-Britt says. She's part of a project called Green Buds. I smile, and Maj-Britt quickly rolls her eyes. It's in moments like these that I feel we truly understand one another. They won't protrude, will they, I ask. Maj-Britt guarantees they won't, because she's sewn them herself. Bent is in the kitchen boiling a pot of pork ribs. It's his favorite dish, but the disadvantage is that they are messy to eat. He lifts two small ribs out of the pot and puts them on a saucer, which he passes over to me. My son stands up with his hands on my knees, and he looks on with interest as I bite the bone. Like most people, I eat the same way I have sex. In my case, it's ugly and unrestrained but with the greatest enthusiasm, I say, and I dry my mouth with a sheet of paper towel. I say that I hope they have a good weekend. It's Tuesday, May-Britt says. Her voice comes from within the refrigerator. You know what I mean, I say, and I put my son's bike helmet on. Maybe, Maj-Britt says.

ANDERS AGGER AND I are drinking the remnants from opened bottles in the wine cellar of Hotel Skjern, while Krisser collects used glasses on a tray and rolls up some Irish flags. Do you want a kidney for the road, she says, and she puts a platter in front of us. We take one each and Anders Agger says that there's nothing quite like entrails. Lend me your expertise, I say to him, and do a voiceover for my life. Krisser opens a window, and asks him to do it in his TV voice. He is contacted regularly by people planning bachelor parties or just playing practical jokes on their friends. They send a homemade manuscript, and Anders Agger reads it and sends a sound file back. He clears his throat and looks at me in concentration. What is time, Anders Agger says, but random intervals of joy and fear, country roads stretching out before us, and heavy traffic in Herning. One morning you'll wake up, says Anders Agger, drive down the pedestrian street, and execute a perfect parallel parking job in front of Italia. Suddenly it will all make sense, like falling in love unexpectedly in a deserted land. You let a new generation pull past you, and you understand that to have a child is to pass on the things you love in the hands of reality. You have a great responsibility: that your busy days, your sorrows and mistakes, will compose another person's childhood. It feels like sitting behind the wheel and slamming the door shut. You put your seatbelt on, start the engine, and hope for the best. You look out for dangerous intersections, loose gravel, black ice, steep declines, roadwork, sudden traffic jams, and wild animals in the forests. You know that there are dangers lurking, endless roundabouts, but there are also parking spaces that appear out of nowhere. There are wheels on the road, wings in the wind, and, like a connect-the-dot puzzle, you move between three points: the advice column, the cars, and the child. You know you must learn to love traffic, Anders Agger says, that magnificent organism that lives at the intersection of wariness and trust. A constant buzz of speeding movements dancing across the globe, a living being swirling in and out, between cities and countries. You will understand the beauty of the system, the symmetry of the highways, the chaotic order, and that everyone you meet is on the way somewhere. Bravo, I say, and Anders Agger says thank you.

Dear Letterbox,

I am a young woman and at the end of summer I'll become the mother of a baby boy. He was conceived on a balcony in Greece, with a view of the sea and the mountains. Because of the due date, I had decided to call him August, but I've just found out that Balcony would be a legally permissible name. I think naming my son Balcony would be a whimsical twist and a fun story, but my parents are against it, and they asked me if I had a heat stroke.

Sincerely,

The Girl with the Interrail Pass

Dear Heat Stroke,

This time it's going to be a little bit about me, because I know how hard it is to find the right name. My son was over a year and half old before we decided on a name for him, but like so much else, it seemed far more important than it actually was. Behind every driver's license there is a superhero, and mine is called Parking Peter. He has a cat called Frode, and, because Parking Peter and his family live along a highway, it isn't a rare occurrence that Frode gets run over and killed. Then they get a new cat, which they call Frode, until the process repeats. I very much admire this unsentimental cat replacement. It's as if the name is the pet and not the cat. Dear Heat Stroke, your child shouldn't be called Balcony. Just because something is legal doesn't necessarily make it a good idea. I suggest that you call your little one Peter instead.

Warm regards,

The Letterbox

SEBASTIAN AND I are sitting in an oversized Postman Pat car with our children on our laps. There's an infernal noise coming from the bouncy castle, and a little girl throws some big rubber insects down at us from the climbing wall. A flying spider hits me in the neck when I go get a tray with juice boxes and french fries. My son and Freja dip the fries thoroughly in remoulade and start throwing them at Sebastian and me, laughing. They rile each other up like two wild animals, and when we take the food away, they both scream, holding short pauses to breathe at exactly the same intervals. Is there some sort of pill that could pacify them, I ask. Sebastian nods and runs off to get a bag of gummy candies. Afterward, we put the children in the cozy corner. They take turns hitting one another over the head with a copy of *Grimms' Fairy Tales*, but on the whole they seem to have calmed down. Sebastian draws a deep breath and passes me a cup of coffee. There was a time when I didn't understand why parents were always talking about their children, but now I've realized that it's not because we are happy, but because we are in shock. We are stunned by our subjugation. It's impossible to imagine until you've been a witness to your own downfall. Sebastian is a crutch that I cling to in Bork Playland. We are friends and allies, we are slaves to our children, and we want a union. Loud howls erupt because my son and Freja both want to wear the same tiara. Sebastian claps his hands and asks if anyone wants to hear the story of Little Red Riding Hood and the Protruding Wolf, and they come crawling toward us, still enraged, but also curious. Is this really what we

want to be doing with our lives, I ask Sebastian. Yes, he
says, believe it or not.

DO YOU DUST your houseplants, I ask Maj-Britt as I step out of my rubber boots. She is gently running a damp cloth over each leaf, which she does every Wednesday. Does the municipality make you do this too, I ask. No, this is a personal requirement, says Maj-Britt, and she puts a platter of pastries in front of me. I have a problem with self-control, I say between two muffins. There's more where that came from, Maj-Britt says, and she points to the kitchen counter, where they are lined up in three even rows. There's a knock at the door and Nor's mother comes in to the kitchen with her four children. Maj-Britt passes the platter of muffins over to them. Nor's mother praises their consistency in the highest terms, and says no when her eldest reaches for one more. I look down at the four muffin liners that are lying balled up on my plate. It's because I have my period, I say. Nor's mother knows the feeling. You're a little hungry all the time, she says. I tell them how my boyfriend gives me a carrot when I say that I'm hungry. A carrot, I say, and I look at Maj-Britt as she pours more lemonade in my mug. Carrots are good for digestion, Nor's mother says. Digestion, I say, I'm not digesting, I'm bleeding. I want chips or chocolate, french fries with mayonnaise, cream puffs and raspberry bars, white bread with a thick layer of butter and béarnaise sauce. A carrot, I say, it's just insane. Nor's mother's children agree. If my boyfriend were employed at a twenty-four-hour pharmacy and had a shotgun up against his forehead, he would amicably and confidently hand the drug addict a pack of Tylenol. No more than six per day, my boyfriend would say, and remember to take them with a big glass of water. It's good that your husband looks after your health, Nor's mother says. They aren't married, Maj-Britt says. You can divide all lovers into two groups, I say, those who save, and those who need saving. It might sound rigid, but that is the true order of the world. Nor's mother says there might be something to it. I've never tried to save anyone, I say, which fortunately has meant that, throughout my love life, I've been surrounded by upright and relatively harmonious people. People who lay out their groceries barcode-up so the cashier doesn't have to search for it, and who hang small green balls of seed in the trees for the birds. Yin and yang, Maj-Britt says, and she starts folding up a pile of cloth diapers. But don't forget, I say, raising my index finger, that they get a rush out of it. Superheroes are superfluous without catastrophes, a bouncer needs a club, a doctor needs people to cut up. From the outside, I might look like the unreasonable one, I say, but it's just a question of attitude. If I left my boyfriend, three days wouldn't go by before his bed would be transformed into a dark cave where he would sit and smoke cigarettes and eat hot dogs while desperately trying to download the newest version of Civilization. His social life would drop dead, and, as if it were the only way out, he would curl up in the fetal position and watch pornography in a compulsive and sorrowful fashion. He would eat gummy bears, first the red ones, then the green ones, then the yellow ones, and then he would call the grocery store and have them deliver a new supply. One day would turn into the next, until one morning when he would hear a crunching in the gravel as a psychologically unstable woman rode by on her bicycle. Then his ears would prick up, something inside of him would awaken. He would experience the warm sensation of someone calling out for him in need, and he would answer that call in search of the same. Relieved, he would get up, pick up the vacuum cleaner, and possibly even take a shower. When he opened the door for this rattling bundle of nerves, he would be caring, but also grateful. And the grotesque thing is, I say, that if this woman came home one day with a hot dog, then he would tell her that he had just been out shopping for a vegetarian dish with cabbage and prunes. If she ever opened a tiny bag of gummy bears, then he would say, we're eating soon, but take a carrot if you're hungry. You've got to meet in the middle, Maj-Britt says. But I say that I prefer the corners of the ring. What is a compromise if not two people who are both unsatisfied in their own way. What is death, I say, but an incessant stream of wedding invitations. Bent says you should just find yourself someone from West Jutland. Such reliable spouses, I say, and Maj-Britt nods.

Dear Letterbox,

We are a couple in the beginning of our thirties, who met one another when we were university students. It feels like we are drifting further and further away from our friends from back then, and we don't really know why. Most of us have had children over the past couple of years, and even though being in the same life situation ought to strengthen our friendships, that hasn't been the case at all. It seems like everyone wants to show off how well they are doing, even though it's obvious that things aren't perfect. Should we delete our Facebook profiles? Do you think that would make our relationships more honest?

Sincerely,

The Friends

Dear Friends,

I'll be the first to admit that my age brings out something undignified in me, but I also see it as a generational problem. We are victims of the joyless intoxication of our thirties, we are rough seas, waves blindly following the current. I detest all the small, self-righteous families that shoot up like weeds, the automatic jubilation, the triumph that shines out of their baby carriages like laser beams. The ugly wooden toys, the homemade broccoli puree, the songs we sing. The fragile earnestness of our efforts, all the things we do for the first time. We've been acting it out in games of make-believe since preschool and now we're repeating it all, with the foolish innocence of a child, and a grown-up's fear of loss. We take a close look at one another, our peer nations. We check the employment statistics, the treasury, and the population's happiness levels. My son had a phase when he was seven months old, which started out of the blue, where he wouldn't let me out of his sight. Have you had that, my boyfriend and I asked a couple we are friends with. No, they hadn't, because they had always made it a priority that their child should have a close bond with both of them. They were glad they hadn't had to go through it, they thought it sounded hard, and they said they had been lucky with their child, who was equally bonded with them both. Perhaps this was because, from the start, they had made a big effort to ensure the mother was not the primary caregiver. How could she be, I thought, when the children spend eighty percent of their childhood in a daycare institution. We're lucky that our jobs are flexible, my boyfriend said, and we started complimenting ourselves about how early our son gets picked up. Long mornings, I said, we think they're extremely important. I don't actually know if I think they are important, I've just always had a hard time getting out the door, but I know that I wanted to be lucky, and I wanted to be luckier than them. Our friend's daughter sniffled a little. They had a hard time acclimating her to her daycare, she was sick for almost a month, one infection followed the next with an impressive tempo, raging around in her little body. Isn't it crazy, my boyfriend said, that our son is never sick. Knock on wood, I said, and we smiled to each other. For reasons I cannot possibly understand, we are incredibly proud of our son's health, and we can talk about it for hours if no one interrupts us. It must be because we're not so paranoid about him getting a little dirty, we said, if not in unison then at least in concert. Then came the bit about how our son sits out in the garden and eats sand and leaves, and how we think that bacteria is natural, and how you can see the results with your own eyes. Never sick, and color in his cheeks, not to mention that he's a certified child of nature, we said, cackling loud and shrill. Getting together with our friends is humiliating. We've become one another's intimate enemies, like a mirror where I check my hair and my hair always looks awful. If our life choices are not completely identical, it feels like an accusation, and a ghost of arrogance and insecurity sits alongside us at every dinner. Once, my friends were a room I could go into and scream, loud and long. Now, we imitate affection like braindead parrots. This weekend I was at a dinner party with my old German teacher, who had just turned forty-five, and suddenly I was filled with hope. You're not divorced, the guests asked, well, then you should be. Their eyes shone, they slept at night, and they had stopped putting on any kind of act. Their attempts at nest building had ground to a halt in the middle of the sunroom, and there was something erotic about them. Dear Friends, the only people in their thirties who get along well with their friends are in TV shows, the rest of us have to gather our wits before we can meet again in our forties. See you on the other side.

Warm regards,

The Letterbox

THE HØJSKOLE HAS fallen into its ritual collective depression because the students will soon be going home. You'd think they'd be able to see it coming, as it happens every year, Sebastian says, but his wife is just as crushed every time. Early that morning she was picked up by the ceramics teacher, who stood outside their door with red puffy eyes, looking traumatized. They all went down in a flock to write their names on the windmill. They clung to one another and watched the sun rise. Both of the children woke up and Sebastian was alone with them for two hours before their daycares opened. But despite that, the thing that annoyed him most was the tearful rendition of Look, the Sun Is Rising that he could hear all the way up in their kitchen. There is a farewell party at the school, and the principal has made it clear that the trailing spouses are expected to attend. You are also part of the school's story, the principal wrote in the invitation to the teachers' partners. There are high spirits, but also sorrow, because the moment of farewell approaches. A tall guy walks around crying in a pink fleece costume with rabbit ears, and three teachers go up and hug him at the same time. Sebastian looks at me and raises his bottle of beer. During the dinner, one speech follows the next, and I can hardly hear what's been said before people start laughing or loudly weeping. You all have made many new impressions and many new expressions, the ceramics teacher says as she cries. She says that she's never had a group of students with so few failed raku firings. And we haven't had any problems with dried-out clay on the tools, or dirty pottery wheels. You have shown responsibility, she says, her voice cracking. The little group of students with purple wigs on starts crying. The organic nutrition teacher holds a speech addressed to the planet. In the end we are each other, she says. We may carve our names into the bark now, but one day the trees will cut us back. The last event of the night is the awards show. My boyfriend wins the golden dick for being the hottest teacher at the school. His face turns red as he accepts it, and he looks down at the floor. Three of the writing students, wearing transparent dresses, hand him the statue. I stand up on a chair and wave my hands. How about giving me the golden pussy, I yell, you should get one for giving birth to a child. The principal says that they could definitely introduce this category, that she's always happy for new input. My boyfriend takes his golden dick back to his seat while the principal pours more red wine into my glass. Emma and Malte walk onto the stage and they grant me the title of oracle of the year. They read short passages from my advice column into the microphone while a little film plays on the big screen with clips of my attempts to park in front of the højskole. They call me up to the stage, and I receive a crystal ball made of paper-mache. When the lobes of your brain finish growing together in a few years, you'll slowly start to understand what it's all about, I say, and I adjust the microphone. You think that youth is a character trait, I yell. You wander around in one another's dreams so seriously, as if they were reality itself. Time makes no mark on you, it's just an endless plain for you to cartwheel across. Not only do you live in the present, you are the present, and that is why we love you. You charm us with your smooth skin and your clear eyes, but we have a knowledge that we keep secret from you. One day your skin will start to loosen from your bones, wrinkles will draw themselves across your faces, and your hair will gradually grow thin. Dear youth, I say, getting older is nice, but life also becomes more tame. You get fixed in your routines, and you surrender the spotlight to others, with a tired wave of the hand. Your sharpness disappears, your pores get bigger, your body falls into place in soft folds, not because it gives up, but because it finds peace. Bravo, yells the principal, and people start clapping. The dancefloor fills up, and from the loudspeakers come long vibrating tones from Sebastian's ceramic bowl. Our son has fallen asleep between two chairs, and we lift him carefully into the baby carriage. In the early summer morning, we hear the rooks calling from down by the fjord and we make our way toward our little red house. The neighbor's horse begins to neigh as the first train passes under the bridge, and it is here we go home, amid all these horizons, while Velling wakes.

The Land of Short Sentences
Hymn

Melody: Dear Line Dancer (Kære linedanser)
Composer: Per Krøis Kjærsgaard, 1998

1 Dear flatlands, far from the sky
   wild west of the north
   like a knight
   at dawn's first light
   on my horse I venture forth.

   While I tilt at windmills here
   and try to settle down
   the wind never stands still
   it blows me all around.

   If you want to, you can learn
   to love
   the land of short sentences
   a language of water, earth, and wind.

2 The country road stretches before me
   like an eternity
   long commitments
   and deep ditches
   as vast as the sea.

The wind whistles within us
and it has no brakes
when the others slow down
every car we overtake.

But when the crows turn around
and see
the crooked, dancing trees
that's where their nest is meant to be.

3 Dear youth, listen closely
listen to my song
your future dreams
far though they seem
will be yours before long.

Trust now in my love for you
for although it is tired
the fjord is full, yes it is true
of all tears we've cried.

Behind a meeting stands a parting
it waves
and hums softly to itself
when the time has come to say farewell.

4 On a highway of memories
we walk into the blue
headlights burning
new friends learning
who they're talking to.

We're the children of the wind
and when you go away

remember that like birds in flight
we are not here to stay.

Every one of us is a leaf
in the wind
so randomly thrust
and here we are in the same gust.

TRANSLATOR'S NOTES

HØJSKOLE: The højskole was conceptualized in Denmark in the 19th century as an accessible, liberal alternative to the strict preparatory schools of the time. A great many of them were established, and they remain an important part of Danish education and culture generally. Højskole is attended mostly by young adults looking to deepen their skills in a certain field (e.g.: arts, music, sports, or design), but the humanistic and communitarian underpinnings remain. N. F. S. Grundtvig, leader of the højskole movement, had the following to say about them: "This is not a school for little children that we are starting, but what we are calling an adult *højskole*. And yet we shall have to tell these adults much of what they should actually have learned in school when they were children, because they did not hear it at the time." (Translated by Anders Holm)

THE SONGS: There is a strong tradition of group singing in Denmark, and one of the forms it takes is the *lejlighedssang* or "occasional song." In a lejlighedssang, original lyrics are written for a specific occasion (often a wedding or a birthday) and set to well-known melodies so that everyone can sing along. The songs in *The Land of Short Sentences* could be considered lejlighedssange, as many Danish readers would be able to sing along while reading the lyrics. Group singing also plays a big role in højskole culture, and a Højskole Songbook is published every year with new songs added in. In fact, the 2020 Højskole Songbook included four of Stine Pilgaard's songs from *The Land of Short Sentences*. While reading the lyrics, you can listen to the melodies they were written to and experience lejlighedssange for yourself. On the World Editions YouTube channel you can also find the English version of the title song, "The Land of Short Sentences," performed by Leah Uijterlinde.

FJORD: Ringkøbing Fjord is not technically a fjord but a lagoon, and although Denmark has a number of actual fjords, they are not of the dramatic, mountainous variety that most English language readers will likely imagine. Rather, they are lined with rolling hills, and sometimes the surrounding landscape is completely flat. It should be noted that the landscape around Ringkøbing Fjord (which, again, is not really a fjord) is of the latter variety. Despite its more grandiose associations, we elected to stick with the word "fjord" in the translation, partly out of faith to the place-name, partly to show the word's versatility in its native linguistic setting, and partly because it is a nice word.

HUNTER SIMPSON is originally from North Carolina and currontly lives in Copenhagen, Denmark. Stine Pilgaard's *The Land of Short Sentences* is his first published literary translation.

On the Design

As book design is an integral part of the reading experience, we would like to acknowledge the work of those who shaped the form in which the story is housed.

Tessa van der Waals (Netherlands) is responsible for the cover design, cover typography, and art direction of all World Editions books. She works in the internationally renowned tradition of Dutch Design. Her bright and powerful visual aesthetic maintains a harmony between image and typography and captures the unique atmosphere of each book. She works closely with internationally celebrated photographers, artists, and letter designers. Her work has frequently been awarded prizes for Best Dutch Book Design.

Internationally renowned Dutch illustrator Annemarie van Haeringen got her inspiration for the cover illustration from the title of the book. She saw a staccato series of short sentences before her, and captured that in her little icon-like drawings dotted around the cover. Bodega Sans Light Oldstyle is an Art Deco–inspired font designed by Greg Thompson. Our designer Tessa van der Waals chose it in part because of the playful little lowercase *g* and the characteristic capital *S*, which appears three times on the cover.

The cover has been edited by lithographer Bert van der Horst of BFC Graphics (Netherlands).

Suzan Beijer (Netherlands) is responsible for the typography and careful interior book design of all World Editions titles.

The text on the inside covers and the press quotes are set in Circular, designed by Laurenz Brunner (Switzerland) and published by Swiss type foundry Lineto.

All World Editions books are set in the typeface Dolly, specifically designed for book typography. Dolly creates a warm page image perfect for an enjoyable reading experience. This typeface is designed by Underware, a European collective formed by Bas Jacobs (Netherlands), Akiem Helmling (Germany), and Sami Kortemäki (Finland). Underware are also the creators of the World Editions logo, which meets the design requirement that "a strong shape can always be drawn with a toe in the sand."